Praise for Ray K
and His Thrillers & N

"A riveting entry in a multivolume series that continues to deliver strong characters and suspense."

- Kirkus Reviews on *Vatican Shadows*

"Exciting, tightly written action scenes comprise the final act, but there's humor sprinkled throughout the narrative, as well... A short but kinetic tale featuring a consistently entertaining hero."

- Kirkus Reviews on *The Traitor*

"...an addictively entertaining five-star read."

- BookViral Reviews on *Cathedral*

"My grade for this series went up... As of this writing, it is an A and let me tell you, it sometimes leans upwards towards the A+. It is really good! As spy books go, it has lots and lots of action. It has a whole lot more thinking than most genre books do. It definitely has more actual preaching (sermons) and prayers. Most importantly, it has a ton of humanity."

- SpyGuysandGals.com

"A fast-paced, exuberant outing for the virtuoso clergyman and his numerous comrades."

- Kirkus Reviews on *Deep Rough*

"... a page-turning and unpredictable ride, and a firm foundation for Keating's enticing new series."

- Self-Publishing Review, ★★★★
on *Cathedral*

"A hugely entertaining thriller... Typically underpinned by Keating's extensive religious and historical research, *Under the Golden Dome* is richly layered in a way that puts more conventional thrillers to shame... A highly enjoyable, intelligent and thought-provoking read, *Under the Golden Dome* is unreservedly recommended."

- BookViral Reviews, ★★★★★

"Mr. Keating knows how to tell an exciting story. And these books, like the James Bond novels, are ridiculously entertaining. As for larger themes, there is vocation, of course. I see these books as honoring the pastoral ministry. Because in real life, pastors are heroes engaged in saving the world."

- Gene Veith
"Cranach: The Blog of Veith"

"It was my great privilege that Ronald Reagan and I were good friends and political allies. This exciting political thriller may be a novel but it truly captures President Reagan's optimism and principles."

- Ambassador Fred J. Eckert on *Reagan Country*

"First-rate supporting characters complement the sprightly pastor, who remains impeccable in this thriller."

- *Kirkus Reviews* on *Lionhearts*

"Keating does an excellent job, as usual, integrating heady concepts and moving his recklessly intense plot forward, and the dialogue is snappy, believable, and purposeful. All told, this is another strong installment in a series that always delivers."

- *Self-Publishing Review* on *Under the Golden Dome*

"Keating has accumulated an impressive assortment of characters in his series, and he gives each of them ample opportunity to shine... As in the preceding novels, the author skillfully blends Grant's sermonizing with intermittent bouts of violence. It creates a rousing moral quandary for readers to ponder without either side overwhelming the storyline. Tight action scenes complement the suspense (uncertainty over when the next possible attack will be) ... The villains, meanwhile, are just as rich and engrossing as the good guys and gals. The familiar protagonist, along with sensational new and recurring characters, drives an energetic political tale."

- Kirkus Reviews on *Reagan Country*

"Grant is a selfless and fascinating protagonist. Keating pulls back the walls of the pastor's psyche and lets readers root around, providing a sense of intimacy and closeness with the central character from very early on in the novel. *Warrior Monk* is full of intentional, thoughtful writing that hits hard and carries the story to the end. After devouring this opening salvo, new fans will dive in eagerly to the future adventures of Pastor Stephen Grant."

- Self-Publishing Review, ★★★★½, on *Warrior Monk*

"Author Ray Keating delivers a timely, high-octane, and well-penned thriller with his latest novel, *The Traitor*. The inimitable Pastor Stephen Grant must unexpectedly navigate the shadowy waters of international espionage to keep his country safe and strong. With a gripping plot that feels torn from last week's headlines, Keating knows how to capture his readers immediately and never let go. Pastor Grant continues to surprise as a character and the dialogue hums with authenticity, making the newest Pastor Stephen Grant Novel another hit in this ever-growing series."

- Self-Publishing Review, ★★★★½, on *The Traitor*

"A first-rate mystery makes this a series standout..."

"The author packs a lot into this frantically paced novel... a raft of action sequences and baseball games are thrown into the mix. The multiple villains and twists raise the stakes... Action fans will find plenty to love here, from gunfights and murder sprees to moral dilemmas."

"Ray Keating is a great novelist."

"A gritty, action-stuffed, well-considered thriller with a gun-toting clergyman."

"I miss Tom Clancy. Keating fills that void for me."

"President Ronald Reagan's legacy will live on in the U.S., around the world and in the pages of history. And now, thanks to Ray Keating's *Reagan Country*, it will live on in the world of fiction. *Reagan Country* ranks as a page-turning thriller that pays homage to the greatest president of the twentieth century."

"The plot is vigorously paced, crammed with vividly depicted action and drama... the reader is never lost in this accessible tale of international intrigue."

"Mr. Keating's storytelling is so lifelike that I almost thought I had worked with him when I was at Langley. Like the fictitious pastor, I actually spent 20 years working for the U.S. intelligence community, and once I started reading *The River*, I had to keep reading because it was so well-crafted and easy to follow and because it depicted a personal struggle that I knew all too well. I simply could not put it down."

"Keating's creativity and storytelling ability remain on point, for a fun and different take on Pastor Grant, and one that's just as satisfying as longer books in the series."

"Ray Keating has a knack for writing on topics that could be pulled from tomorrow's headlines."

"Must read for any Reaganite."

"A first-class thriller and an uncompromising five-star read!"

"Pastor Grant continues to be one of the most entertaining heroes in the political thrillers and suspense genre. With occasional pop-ins from fan-favorite recurring characters, *Deep Rough* fits in perfectly with the rest of the series – quirky, tightly woven, and difficult to put down. Keating manages to keep his writing fresh and surprising with every new Pastor Grant book. This series satisfies yet again, finding unique ways to entertain and enlighten along the way."

"*Root of All Evil?* is an extraordinarily good read. Only Ray Keating could come up with a character like Pastor Stephen Grant."

"*The Traitor* is a game-changer for the *Warrior Monk* series starring Pastor Stephen Grant. It is in many ways a return to the worldbuilding Ray Keating did with *Warrior Monk,* and is an excellent jumping on point for new readers."

"This gripping tale of deception, retribution, and redemption is filled with espionage, action, and a good deal of enticing mystery. Keating's original twists and singular protagonist result in another solid ride."

"Thriller and mystery writers have concocted all manner of main characters, from fly fishing lawyers to orchid aficionados and former ballplayers, but none has come up with anyone like Stephen Grant, the former Navy Seal and CIA assassin, and current Lutheran pastor. Grant mixes battling America's enemies and sparring with enemies of traditional Christian values, while ministering to his Long Island flock. The amazing thing is that the character works. The Stephen Grant novels are great reads beginning with *Warrior Monk*, which aptly describes Ray Keating's engaging hero."

- David Keene
The Washington Times

"This condensed mystery is enjoyably gripping, and marked by the author's characteristic style of suspense."

- *Self-Publishing Review* on *Past Lives*

"*Warrior Monk* by Ray Keating has all of the adventure, intrigue, and believable improbability of mainstream political thrillers, but with a lead character, Pastor Stephen Grant, that resists temptation."

- *Lutheran Book Review* on
Warrior Monk

"This is a fantastic novel... If you are a comic book fan who is fed up with the political correctness that's going on, you have got to pick up *Heroes and Villains*... I highly recommend this book."

- Jacob Airey, host of *StudioJake*

FOR BETTER, FOR WORSE

A Pastor Stephen Grant Short Story

RAY KEATING

This book is a work of fiction. Names, characters, places, events and incidents either are the product of the author's imagination or are used fictitiously. Any resemblance to actual persons, living or dead, events or locales is entirely coincidental.

For more information:
Keating Reports LLC
raykeating@keatingreports.com

ISBN-13: 9798851039379

Cover design by Jonathan Keating.

For
Beth,
Jonathan
and
Mikayla, David & Phoebe

Previous Books by Ray Keating

Under the Golden Dome: A Pastor Stephen Grant Novel (2023)

Persecution: A Pastor Stephen Grant Novel (2022)

Cathedral: An Alliance of Saint Michael Novel (2022)

What's Lost? A Pastor Stephen Grant Short Story (2021)

Past Lives: A Pastor Stephen Grant Short Story (2021)

Vatican Shadows: A Pastor Stephen Grant Novel (2020)

Root of All Evil? A Pastor Stephen Grant Novel
(Second Edition, 2020)

The Traitor: A Pastor Stephen Grant Novel (2019)

Deep Rough: A Pastor Stephen Grant Novel (2019)

Warrior Monk: A Pastor Stephen Grant Novel
(Second Edition, 2019)

Shifting Sands: A Pastor Stephen Grant Short Story (2018)

Heroes & Villains: A Pastor Stephen Grant Short Story (2018)

Reagan Country: A Pastor Stephen Grant Novel (2018)

Lionhearts: A Pastor Stephen Grant Novel (2017)

Wine Into Water: A Pastor Stephen Grant Novel (2016)

Murderer's Row: A Pastor Stephen Grant Novel (2015)

The River: A Pastor Stephen Grant Novel (2014)

An Advent for Religious Liberty:
A Pastor Stephen Grant Novel (2012)

Root of All Evil? A Pastor Stephen Grant Novel (2012)

Warrior Monk: A Pastor Stephen Grant Novel (2010)

In the nonfiction arena...

The Weekly Economist II: 52 More Quick Reads to Help You
Think Like an Economist (2023)

The Lutheran Planner: The TO DO List Solution (2022)

The Weekly Economist:
52 Quick Reads to Help You Think Like an Economist (2022)

"The Christian is supposed to love his neighbor, and since his wife is his nearest neighbor, she should be his deepest love."

- Martin Luther

"In sharp contrast with our culture, the Bible teaches that the essence of marriage is a sacrificial commitment to the good of the other."

- Timothy Keller, *The Meaning of Marriage*

"Revenge proves its own executioner."

- John Ford, director

"Ah, Kirk, my old friend. Do you know the Klingon proverb that tells us revenge is a dish that is best served cold?"

- Khan, *Star Trek: The Wrath of Khan*

Brief Dossiers on Recurring Characters

Pastor Stephen Grant. After college, Grant joined the Navy, became a SEAL, and went on to work at the CIA. He subsequently became a Lutheran pastor, serving at St. Mary's Lutheran Church on the eastern end of Long Island. He also works on an initiative known as the Lutheran Response to Christian Persecution. Grant grew up in Ohio, just outside of Cincinnati. He possesses a deep knowledge of theology, history, and weapons. His other interests include archery, golf, movies, the beach, poker and baseball, while also knowing his wines, champagnes and brews. Stephen Grant is married to Jennifer Grant.

Jennifer Grant. Jennifer is a respected, sought-after economist and author. Along with Yvonne Hudson and Joe McPhee, she is a partner in the consulting firm Coast-to-Coast Economics. Her first marriage to then-Congressman Ted Brees ended when the congressman had an affair with his chief of staff. Jennifer loves baseball (a Cardinals fan while her husband, Stephen, cheers on the Reds) and literature, and has an extensive sword and dagger collection. Jennifer grew up in the Las Vegas area, with her father being a casino owner.

Paige Caldwell. For part of Stephen Grant's time at the CIA, Paige Caldwell was his partner in the field and in the bedroom. After Stephen left the Agency, Paige continued with the CIA until she eventually was forced out. However, she went on to start her own firm, CDM International Strategies and Security, with two partners – Charlie Driessen and Sean McEnany.

Charlie Driessen. Charlie was a longtime CIA veteran, who had worked with both Stephen Grant and Paige Caldwell. Driessen left the Agency to work with Paige at CDM. Prior to the CIA, he spent a short time with the Pittsburgh police department.

Sean McEnany. After leaving the Army Rangers, Sean McEnany joined the security firm CorpSecQuest, which was part legitimate business and part CIA front. He later signed up with Caldwell and Driessen at CDM. He maintains close contact with the CIA, and has a secret, high-security office in the basement of his suburban Long Island home, along with a mobile unit disguised as a rather typical van parked in the driveway. McEnany's ability to obtain information across the globe has an almost mystical reputation in national security circles. For good measure, Sean, his wife, Rachel, and their children attend St. Mary's Lutheran Church, where Stephen Grant is pastor.

Rachel McEnany. Rachel met Sean while she worked for the Defense Intelligence Agency. In addition to being a mom, she helps Stephen Grant and others with an initiative known as the Lutheran Response to Christian Persecution.

Father Tom Stone. A priest and rector at St. Bartholomew's Anglican Church on Long Island, Tom is one of Grant's closest friends, and served as Stephen's best man. He enjoyed surfing while growing up in southern California, and is known for an easygoing manner and robust sense of humor. Along with Stephen, Tom and other friends regularly meet for morning devotions and conversation at a local diner, and often play golf together. Tom is married to Maggie Stone, who runs her own public relations business. They are the parents to six children.

Father Ron McDermott. Father McDermott, a priest, was the pastor at St. Luke's Roman Catholic Church and School, where he was a strong and caring leader. He also was part of the morning devotions group of friends at the diner. But he recently took a position at the Vatican, working with Pope Paul VII on assorted matters, including Christian persecution in various parts of the world.

Phil Lucena. Charlie Driessen brought Phil from the CIA to work at CDM. Lucena is well known for his courteousness, as well as expertise in close combat.

Jessica West. Paige Caldwell wooed Jessica away from the FBI to join CDM. West thinks fast and acts accordingly. She has suffered major losses, with her father and brother, both Marines, dying in Afghanistan and Iraq, respectively, and her then-fiancé, a fellow FBI agent, perishing in a terrorist attack in New York City. She came to work at CDM in part to dispense a kind of harsh justice that would not have been possible with the FBI. She also excels at beach volleyball.

Chase Axelrod. Chase worked with Sean McEnany at CorpSecQuest, and then became an employee of CDM. He grew up in Detroit, became a star tight end with a 4.0 grade point average in college, and then earned a master's degree in foreign languages from N.C. State. He has mastered six foreign languages – Mandarin, German, French, Russian, Spanish and Japanese – and continues to work on others.

Kent Holtwick. Paige Caldwell invited Kent to leave the Secret Service to join CDM. He has expertise in the area of finance, and excels in the field. His interests include minor league baseball.

Brooke Semmler. When Paige Caldwell invited Kent Holtwick to leave the Secret Service to work at CDM, she did the same for Kent's partner, Brooke. In addition to being adept in the field, Semmler possesses a near-encyclopedic knowledge of international politics. She also calls herself a "theme park enthusiast."

Edward "Tank" Hoard. Tank Hoard has risen through the ranks of the CIA. He worked with Stephen Grant while Grant was at the Agency. Hoard is a bodybuilder, who also happens to be well-educated and skilled at managing people and politics at the CIA.

President Adam Links. Links graduated West Point at the top of his class, and was awarded the Bronze Star while serving in the first Gulf War. He left the military when his wife was diagnosed with pancreatic cancer. After her death, Links joined and buried himself in the CIA, where he had a secret relationship with Paige Caldwell. After leaving the CIA, he came out of nowhere to win a U.S. Senate seat from Louisiana, and later was picked to be the vice-presidential running mate for Elizabeth Sanderski. He subsequently won his own full term as president, and has renewed his relationship with Paige.

Due Tran. Tran was a Vietnamese contact for Stephen Grant and Paige Caldwell during their CIA days, and recently accepted Paige's invitation to work at CDM.

Chapter 1

"Five below zero. You've got to be kidding me." Charlie Driessen's voice was barely audible in the bitter wind.

"Does it actually feel worse if we think about it in Celsius? In that case, it's 21 below," replied Phil Lucena.

Driessen rolled his eyes. "Who the hell lives here?"

"Do you mean on the islands, in Helsinki or Finland in general?"

"All of the above."

Some of the snow stuck to Driessen's mustache, but the flakes seemed to find a home in Lucena's fluffy brown beard. Indeed, facial skin and hair were the only parts of each person exposed directly to the elements. Boots, heavy pants, and thick coats with fur-lined hoods were the dress of the day.

Jeff Oakes asked, "Do you two always complain like this?"

Lucena answered, "I typically don't." He then tilted his head toward Driessen and shrugged his shoulders.

Driessen replied to Lucena, "So much for your reputation for being so courteous."

"Being polite doesn't mean failing to deal with reality." Lucena thinly smiled.

Driessen looked at his two CIA colleagues and grunted.

Oakes laughed, which countered his saggy look. He was bald, but had thick eyebrows and a beard. He also was slightly overweight, and while nearly six feet tall, his overall droopiness made him appear shorter. Oakes said, "You know, many people find beauty in this. And since being stationed here at the embassy, it's grown on me."

Driessen commented, "Good for you?"

The three looked out at the ice and snow covering the waters at the entrance of Helsinki's South Harbor and beyond into the Gulf of Finland. They stood on a ferry making the short but breathtaking journey from Helsinki to the fortress island of Suomenlinna, or the "Castle of Finland."

The ice seemed to groan as the ferry cut through it. Harbor tugs worked to keep the ice free enough for the ferry and other floating vessels to make their way into and out of the harbor. The floating chunks of ice created fascinating and ever-changing patterns on the water.

Dusk had arrived, and February's full darkness would soon follow.

A small car waited for them near the main pier of Iso Mustasaari island on the north side of Suomenlinna. While a car-free zone, service vehicles were allowed on the islands. Oakes had secured the car, for a not insubstantial bribe, from the small hotel on Suomenlinna.

The meeting was at the actual fortress at the southern point on Kustaanmiekka island.

The three were scheduled to meet a contact who pledged to name and provide the location of an arms dealer the CIA, MI-6 and other national intelligence agencies knew existed, but whose identity had remained a mystery. The incongruity of meeting in the cold, ice and snow of Finland to learn the identity of an individual supplying arms to Middle East terrorists wasn't lost on any of the three operatives. But each also understood that information often was found in the least-expected places, not to mention from surprising sources.

As Oakes guided the vehicle along narrow, cobblestone streets, Driessen reviewed the plan. "This guy – I assume it's a guy – has us meeting inside the fort. Given that it's dark and freezing, anyone else at this location when we meet is probably a person who should worry us."

Oakes interjected, "True. Our contact wanted remote and the cover of darkness. This place provides both."

The car crossed over a canal on a small bridge connecting Iso Mustasaari island to Kustaanmiekka island.

Lucena, who was in the back seat, said, "At the same time, I'm not crazy about there being no more ferries tonight."

"Neither am I," agreed Driessen.

"It certainly isn't ideal," commented Oakes, "but since this guy appears legit, we play by his rules. This is big. Besides, the apartment is secure, and we'll be on the first ferry in the morning."

Oakes had arranged to have overnight access to an apartment on the island.

While driving at the island's 12 mph speed limit, the car still slid on the snow and ice as Oakes made a turn.

Lucena observed, "About 800 people live here."

Oakes added, "That's the max during the summer months. It's only a small fraction of that this time of year."

As they arrived at the fort, Oakes drove between two stone walls. He parked in a small area that during summer months featured umbrella tables outside a restaurant. He positioned the vehicle close to one of the walls.

The fort had been built by the Swedes in the 18th century as a fortification against the Russians attacking by sea. Nonetheless, in the early 19th century, Sweden lost the Finnish War, with Russia taking control of Finland, including Suomenlinna, in 1808-09. It wasn't until 1918 that Finland achieved independence.

The three men silently checked their weapons.

Oakes said, "Okay, let's move."

As planned, Driessen and Oakes headed to one of the small tunnels that led to the last open area within the fort before the outermost wall and the sea beyond. They proceeded slowly, giving Lucena time to move far to their right. He went up a ramp, seeking a position to look down on the meeting with the sea at his back. As he arrived at the top of the ramp, Lucena pulled out his Glock 20 and dropped onto his belly. He crawled the rest of the way, and the snow and ice actually made that task easier. Lucena stopped when he had a clear view of where they were supposed to meet their contact.

Below, Driessen and Oakes slowly emerged from the tunnel. They took a few steps and stopped.

In a low voice, Driessen asked, "So where is this guy?"

Oakes didn't reply. Nothing moved. All that could be heard was the wind, and the sloshing mix of sea water and ice on the other side of the fort walls. Each man unzipped his coat, and pulled out a Glock.

"Why do I suddenly feel like a sitting duck?" Driessen looked up at the walls.

They waited for nearly five minutes. The wind coming off the sea grew stronger and even more frigid.

Then three figures emerged from one of the arched pathway tunnels in front of Oakes and Driessen. Two men – one wearing a knit hat and the other exposing his face and black hair to the cold – held the third person at gunpoint.

At the same time, two figures stepped forward on top of the wall – at the opposite end from where Lucena was positioned.

Driessen whispered, "Shit."

The black-haired man called out, "You're CIA and you've come for information." It was a statement, not a question. The accent was British.

"Let's not do anything stupid. We can come to an agreement," yelled Oakes over the sound-dampening wind.

"Tardy for that!"

The two men shoved their prisoner to the ground.

Driessen glanced up at the two on the wall. To the right, he spotted a figure moving quickly.

Across from Oakes and Driessen, the black-haired individual began to point his weapon at the CIA contact now sprawled out face down on the ground.

Driessen raised his gun, fired and started moving toward the three men. Oakes seemed surprised, but followed.

*   *   *

Above, on the wall of the fort, just as Driessen had pulled the trigger, Lucena stopped moving along the snow and ice.

He leveled his gun, and fired off three shots at the twosome at the other end of the wall.

One projectile hit home. Given the elements, landing one of those shots not only involved skill, but also a good deal of luck.

The man stumbled, and fell forward. His body crashed onto the ice and stone below.

The second man on the wall watched his comrade fall. He then turned toward the source of the shots.

*   *   *

The assailant donning the knit hat returned fire. One of his shots found a target.

Oakes grunted and tumbled to the snow.

Driessen paused and turned toward Oakes, who called out, "I'm good. Go." The pain in his voice was unmistakable even through the harsh weather.

Driessen declared, "Son of a bitch." He turned back just in time to see the black-haired assailant unloading four shots into the man whom Driessen and Lucena had traveled to Finland to meet. Driessen yelled, "No!" He pressed forward, firing as he went.

*   *   *

Lucena was moving at his target as well. The two men exchanged fire, but the wind, snow and darkness, combined with a limited ability to maintain balance on snow and ice, meant that the shots went astray.

When about ten yards away, Lucena actually hurled his gun at his opponent. The man was so surprised that he lost his balance. The gun bounced off his thick coat harmlessly, and the assailant regained his footing. But by that point, Lucena, who already had pulled out a tactical knife, was on top of the man. The CIA operative drove the blade into the side of the assailant's neck.

As the man's body and blood slid down to the ice and snow, Lucena's eyes focused on activity in the distance. He spotted two figures standing on a waterbus landing, used in warmer seasons, between a docked fishing boat and a small SUV parked nearby.

*   *   *

One of Driessen's shots struck the black-haired murderer. As the man fell, his partner turned and moved through one of the tunnels in the stone wall. Driessen fired at the individual seeking escape, but to no avail.

Getting closer, the black-haired opponent was still moving, attempting to raise his gun. Driessen then deposited two shots into the man's head.

Not far to his left, Lucena actually jumped down from the wall, landing and rolling in the snow. He quickly leaped to his feet, and rushed over to Driessen.

Driessen pointed to one body. "Our contact."

Lucena double-checked for a pulse, but shook his head.

Driessen pointed to the other. "His killer. And a third went through there." He pointed at the archway through which the man had fled.

Lucena declared, "We need to get out of here. There are more. Oakes?"

Driessen started moving toward the third CIA operative who was still lying in the snow. "He's over here."

Oakes said, "The bastard hit my thigh."

"How bad?" asked Driessen.

Oakes answered, "I actually have no idea."

Lucena replied, "Okay. Got to move. We'll get you to the car."

Driessen and Lucena raised up Oakes, who groaned in pain. With an arm around each of his CIA colleagues' shoulders, Oakes was being dragged toward the tunnel where he and Driessen had entered earlier.

As they moved through the tunnel, Driessen asked Oakes, "How do we get out of this?"

"Get to the car. I'll make a call to a last-resort contact. He's costly."

As they arrived at the vehicle, the small van that had been parked at the dock earlier was now coming down the access road the CIA team had used to get to the fort.

Driessen and Lucena basically shoved Oakes into the back seat of the car.

Driessen said, "Get it started." He began firing at the van.

Lucena hopped behind the wheel and started the engine.

Shots were being returned. As Driessen went to follow Oakes into the back seat, a bullet grazed his shoulder. Staggered for a moment, he cursed and then hauled himself into the car. "Go. Go."

Lucena slipped the car into drive, and proceeded to battle the narrow, icy streets, while their pursuers did the same in the van.

Oakes pulled out his cellphone, and hit a number.

A voice answered, "Yes."

Oakes said, "Under the water."

"The fee triples."

"I understand."

The call ended.

Oakes then said, "Head back to the ferry dock." He grimaced. "Pass it by, and take the bridge over to Pikku Mustasaari island."

Lucena replied, "Got it."

Driessen asked, "What the hell are we doing?"

"We're going to drive back to the mainland," answered Oakes.

"How the hell are we going to do that?" demanded Driessen.

Oakes didn't respond immediately, but instead cursed in pain.

As he managed to put some distance between their car and the van chasing them, Lucena asked, "Are you two okay?"

Driessen answered, "Yeah, yeah, just caught my shoulder."

Oakes added, "I haven't bled out yet, so I'm thinking this didn't hit anything vital." He took a deep breath. "There's a service tunnel. It was expanded about 15 years ago so emergency vehicles could get through. Definitely one at a time. It's tight. My contact is going to open the tunnel for us."

"Both ends?" asked Lucena.

"Yeah. He's got someone on the other side."

Driessen commented, "Why doesn't this make me feel confident?"

"You have a better idea?" replied Oakes.

Driessen didn't answer.

Lucena whipped by the ferry entrance, and then entered the small bridge. The car slid, with the wheels hitting the curbed edge of the tiny span. But Lucena kept the vehicle moving forward.

Once on the other island, Oakes directed Lucena, and the door to the tunnel was, in fact, open.

Lucena turned into the entrance. The tunnel descended, and it quickly became otherworldly. Piping ran along one side that handled heating, electricity, water, plumbing and telecommunications services for Suomenlinna. The tunnel was shaped like an arch, and the rock through which it had been cut remained exposed. The lighting provided shadows that made it look even stranger. It was a manmade cave 0.8 miles long and 207 feet below sea level under half rock and half water.

While narrow, it was free from ice and snow. That allowed Lucena to accelerate. It also meant, however, that the van in pursuit could speed up as well.

The ascent began in the tunnel, which meant that they were coming to the exit in Kaivopuisto park in Helsinki.

Lucena declared, "Shit. The door's not open."

"Maybe it's unlocked, and just needs to be pushed open," suggested Driessen.

Lucena stopped the vehicle just 15 yards in front of the door, and Driessen got out of the back seat. He couldn't raise his left arm with the gunshot wound. But he tested and probed everything with his right. "This thing's locked."

He opened a utility box on the wall, discovered a keypad, and called out, "I don't suppose you've got the combination, Oakes?"

Still in the back seat, Oakes cursed in response.

The pursuing van's headlights grew brighter in the tunnel, with the engine sounds getting louder.

Lucena opened his door, and said, "Let's get ready." He moved around to the other side of the door to use it for cover. Driessen did the same on the other side of the vehicle, while Oakes pushed himself up, ready to shoot out and through the rear window.

Lucena said, "Thankfully, I retrieved my gun after I threw it."

While keeping his eyes on the approaching van, Driessen exclaimed, "You threw your gun at one of them?"

"Yes, and it actually worked."

Oakes shot first, with the back window shattering. His shooting was wild, given his position and leg wound.

Driessen concentrated his fire on the passenger side of the van, but he, too, wasn't on his game due to the wounded left shoulder.

The van came to a halt about 20 yards down the tunnel from the CIA group.

Lucena was going to have to make the difference. He targeted the driver as his door opened. Lucena's prey took a projectile in the upper chest, and fell to the cement floor.

But the other two assailants popped their heads up from behind the back doors on both sides of the van. Each assailant stood on the edge of the van's floor and held a machine gun. And when the sprays of bullets were unleashed, all three CIA operatives dropped as low as possible.

Lucena called out, "Oakes, roll onto the floor," and re-entered the car. He threw himself across the driver's seat, and with legs hanging out, Lucena slipped the vehicle into reverse. He used his right hand to push down on the accelerator and placed the other on the steering wheel to keep the car straight. "Hold on!"

The car's rear crashed into the van's grill.

That temporarily stopped the machine gun fire.

Driessen, who followed the car on foot, jumped up on the vehicle's hood. His head was just a few feet short of the rock ceiling. He found a target, and squeezed off three shots.

That left one man with a machine gun, and he got repositioned and pointed the weapon.

Driessen dropped just as a stream of projectiles were sent in his direction. He fell onto the hood, and then tumbled to the tunnel floor.

The bullets stopped as the assailant scanned for targets.

Lucena had crawled along the cement floor, and arrived below the attacker. He raised his Glock, and fired one shot into the man's genitalia. As the target screamed and leaned forward, Lucena deposited another shot between the eyes. The dead man's head slammed into the door as it fell, which directed the body backwards. He came to rest just beyond Lucena's head.

Lucena climbed to his feet. He checked to make sure the driver also was dead. After confirming that, he called out, "Charlie? Jeff? Are you alright?" He heard muffled responses.

Lucena first looked in the back seat at Oakes. The man nodded, and said, "Shit. Thanks."

"You're welcome."

Lucena then went around the car and found Driessen still on the ground.

Driessen said, "My shoulder is a mess, and I think..." He bit his lip. "I think my right wrist is broken."

Lucena said, "Okay..." He was interrupted by the tunnel door clanking. Lucena refocused his weapon at the opening door, as he moved toward it.

A short, fat man stared at the gun.

Lucena yelled, "Hands up, please."

The man raised his hands in the air. "I was supposed to open this, but I was late."

Lucena commanded, "On the ground, if you would. Hands behind your head."

The man did so as quickly as his girth allowed.

Lucena moved past the individual, and scanned the outside area. He re-entered the tunnel, and called out, "Oakes, do you have a code phrase for this guy?"

Oakes called out, "Drive on the ice."

Lucena looked down at the man on the floor. "Well?"

"Yes, yes, um... Oh, okay. I remembered. Um. No one has driven on the ice in years."

Oakes said, "He's good."

Lucena said, "Get up. You have a car?"

"Yes, yes."

"Please, pull it over here as close as you can. We need to get these two to the hospital."

Several months later, CIA headquarters, Langley, Virginia...

Phil Lucena entered Charlie Driessen's small office. "You wanted to see me, Charlie?"

"I'm retiring."

"Excuse me?"

"You heard me."

"I did, but I'm just having a tough time believing it."

Driessen smiled, "I'm not heading to Florida to play golf. I've got an interesting opportunity, and I need a favor from you."

"What can I do?"

"You can come work for me, and for Paige Caldwell."

Chapter 2

A Decade Later...

"I don't want this to sound selfish, but with everything that happened over the past week at Notre Dame and in D.C., heading to California for Jessica and Phil's wedding feels relaxing, almost like a vacation," commented Pastor Stephen Grant.

Jennifer smiled at her husband, and said, "I get it. But you do have work to do, given that you're officiating at the wedding."

"Absolutely, but it's joyous work."

They squeezed each other's hand, and he smiled back at his wife.

Marrying Jen was the best decision of my life, along with becoming a pastor.

Jennifer and Stephen both spoke at a conference at the University of Notre Dame the week before, but a conflict over ideas wound up turning deadly. Now, they were seated next to each other in the main cabin of a Gulfstream G650 jet. The aircraft was touching down at Hollister Municipal Airport just before six on Tuesday evening. The flight from Dulles Airport outside of Washington, D.C., to Hollister, California, had been about five-and-a-half hours, and Stephen enjoyed every moment of the journey.

With Jennifer at his side, they were traveling with a host of friends, including Paige Caldwell and Charlie Driessen, from CDM International Strategies and Security. Caldwell, Driessen, and another CDM staffer, Chase Axelrod, had provided security at the Notre Dame gathering for one of their clients, who happened to be Pope Paul VII. The jet was CDM's ride.

Years earlier, in his previous life at the CIA, Stephen Grant had worked with Caldwell and Driessen – though his relationship with Caldwell back then was much more than merely professional. Now, life found Stephen serving as a pastor at St. Mary's Lutheran Church on eastern Long Island. This week, though, he was jetting to California to officiate at the wedding of good friends and CDM colleagues. On occasion, Stephen still found himself pulled into the CDM sphere, using the skills he'd honed long ago as a SEAL and with the CIA.

During the flight, Stephen and Jennifer were able to get to know better the two most recent additions to the CDM payroll – Ellen Bracken and Jordan Hall. In addition, they caught up with Kent Holtwick and Brooke Semmler.

And while Stephen had chewed the fat with Chase Axelrod during some recent travel, Jennifer and Chase were now able to talk as well.

To top things off, while in the air, Stephen had received a call from his good friend, Father Ron McDermott. Ron relayed news that he was receiving a promotion at the Vatican – to become the pope's secretary of state and a cardinal.

As the landing gear was being lowered, Stephen looked out the window.

You can cover a lot of ground with people during a coast-to-coast flight.

And he appreciated being able to do so. He might be a parish pastor these days, but the CDM team was just as much a part of Stephen's family as his St. Mary's flock.

The G650 rolled slowly into a hangar at the general aviation airport. Three more CDM personnel were waiting inside the hangar next to CDM's second jet.

Due Tran was another more recent staff addition. He had been a CIA contact in Vietnam for Stephen and Caldwell, and after working with them again recently, Tran accepted a position with CDM.

Jessica West and Phil Lucena, of course, were the reason for this Golden State gathering.

As people exchanged greetings, including handshakes and hugs, in the hangar, Jessica West called out, "Excuse me."

Stephen turned to look at a couple who always fascinated him. At six-feet tall, West actually stood four inches taller than Lucena. She had long blond hair, blue eyes, and in addition to working at CDM, she played professional beach volleyball. She seemed to fit the California stereotype, but for her expertise and love of weapons, not to mention an often cutting sense of humor. Meanwhile, Lucena was on the stocky side. His brown hair currently was cut neatly, and accompanied by a beard that came and went apparently with his mood. Lucena was known among this group for unfailing politeness and being lethal in close combat.

West continued, "There are two SUVs outside. We're going to have dinner at one of those nice restaurants in Santa Cruz with a view of the ocean, and then we'll get everyone to where they're staying, whether that be at our place" – she glanced at Lucena – "or at the Sandcastle."

Stephen interrupted, "The Sandcastle?"

Tran responded, "That's what we've been calling the CDM office since we did the expansion."

Caldwell said, "It fits. I like it."

A few minutes later, everyone grabbed places in the two long, silver SUVs that also happened to be armored.

As the vehicles pulled away, a man watching through binoculars from a second floor window in a nearby building pulled out a smartphone. When his call was answered, he reported, "Yes, he's here, too. All of them are now." He listened, and then responded, "Of course, I understand. I'll start things." He spoke with a British accent.

Chapter 3

A table for ten awaited the group in a breezy, Northern California restaurant. All of the seats were on the curve of an arch-shaped table so that each diner had a view of Monterey Bay, the Santa Cruz Wharf, and the Pacific Ocean through the large windows.

The sun had just set, but the sky was alight with colors.

Jennifer leaned over to Stephen, and whispered, "If the food is half as good as the view, this is going to be quite a meal."

In fact, everyone at the table enjoyed the diverse, locally-sourced menu choices.

While his entrée, a tuna steak, was excellent, Stephen had found his almond-crusted mussels appetizer to be a complete delight. Jennifer tried one from the small plate, and immediately declared her disappointment in not ordering it herself.

Stephen paused to appreciate his wife's bliss, with her current smile adding to the beauty of her deep brown eyes, slightly upturned nose, fair skin, and thin frame.

When sharing a meal, Stephen enjoyed the accompanying conversation. But a habit never shaken since his CIA days also was watching people, and trying to pick up on what they were thinking. When honest with himself, he admitted to not really trying to lose the habit. Stephen rather liked the exercise.

Two observations struck him during dinner. The first was catching Caldwell periodically looking in the direction of Jennifer and himself, and at West and Lucena. Grant knew that, even given the many years since they were in a relationship and how much Paige had changed in certain respects, only two people likely knew her better, namely, Charlie Driessen and President Adam Links. And Grant understood probably not in that order, since Caldwell and Links were engaged to eventually get married. That engagement remained a secret to the world, with those aware being people at this table, plus three or four others in or around the White House who were closest to the president.

I wonder if she's thinking about Adam. And could Paige actually be getting impatient about getting married? That would be a change.

Stephen spotted Caldwell looking directly at him with her steely blue eyes. She smirked, and turned away.

The second thing that struck Stephen was related to Lucena and West. Naturally, they were playing hosts, including answering questions about Saturday's wedding and the honeymoon planned for Hawaii. But while people were free to basically sit where they pleased, West made sure that she sat next to Stephen. He wondered why.

The answer came while the main entrée plates were being cleared, and prior to dessert. West leaned over to Stephen, and whispered, "Can you take a moment to talk with Phil and me?"

"Sure."

"Let's step out on the deck."

Stephen followed the couple. The night turned out almost as beautiful as when the sun had set earlier. The breeze, star-populated sky and sound of small waves made for a pleasant combination.

Stephen asked, "So, what's up? Everything okay?"

Lucena and West glanced at each other briefly.

Lucena replied, "Things are great, thank you. We haven't really spoken about this, but with a few people. One of them should've been you earlier than this."

Stephen decided to wait, letting them figure out how to tell him whatever they needed to say.

West cut to the chase. "What you and Pastor Gibson have been talking about regarding marriage, and what it means, actually sank in." West and Lucena joined hands. "So, not long after getting back from the mission in Jordan, we decided to live separately, and you know, sleep separately, until after the wedding."

Stephen found it interesting and distressing that couples today were more awkward about not having sex before they got married, rather than the other way around. He also knew that responding to a couple in such circumstances often amounted to walking a fine line.

He smiled and simply replied, "Well, I'm glad that someone listened to something that Orel and I said." He then added, "No, seriously, I'm glad that's the case. As we've discussed, sex can be a wonderful, beautiful gift, but the Lord means it for the bounds of marriage."

Capturing what Stephen had just been thinking, West rhetorically asked, "Should it really be this awkward? I mean not having sex and having, it seems, to talk about the decision?"

Stephen replied, "Should it be? No. Is it? Well."

Lucena then said, "So, in terms of logistics, Jessica has been staying at a small place that Melissa Ambler has up the coast a bit."

"My matron of honor going above and beyond," added West.

Stephen knew Ambler. She not only ran her late husband's tech-gaming firm, but was a former super model, and operated other ventures, including owning and playing in a beach volleyball league. West and Ambler, in fact, were partners on the sand. Ambler also was a member of St. Bartholomew's Anglican Church back on Long Island, where Father Tom Stone, Stephen's close friend, was rector. Grant thought of Ambler as the woman who did it all, despite her husband, Mike Vanacore, having been murdered. That was burned into Stephen's memory, as he was there when Vanacore had been kidnapped.

"That sounds nice actually, and it'll be good to see Melissa."

West nodded. "She arrives tomorrow night, as will Sean and Rachel."

Sean and Rachel McEnany were flying in from Long Island, and Ambler from southern California. Sean not only was one of the partners that owned CDM, but he, Rachel and their children were members at St. Mary's where Stephen was pastor.

Lucena said, "I wanted Jess to stay at the house, and I'd grab one of the bedrooms at the Sandcastle, but she insisted."

West smiled at her fiancé and said, "Gallantry isn't dead." She kissed his cheek, and added, "But I'm not suffering staying at Melissa's place, to say the least."

The three went back inside just in time to partake in a light dessert.

As the meal was ending, Stephen was back outside. Now, he was taking in the night ocean breeze with Jennifer and Paige. Few things in life made Stephen Grant feel uncomfortable, but one usually was winding up in a setting with just his wife and the person with whom he previously had an intense relationship. Both Jennifer and Paige knew that, and they typically had fun tweaking him. But on this occasion, the three simply enjoyed the relaxed setting and conversation.

Jennifer turned away from the view of the lit up Santa Cruz Wharf, and said, "If you'll excuse me for a moment, I'm going to find the lady's room before we go."

As Jennifer went back inside, Stephen and Paige continued taking in the surroundings.

With her gaze still set on the water, Paige brushed back her long black hair, and said, "And no, Stephen. I saw you wondering. I'm not getting restless about getting married."

"Did I say anything?"

"No, but I could see earlier that you were wondering."

Just in case I forget that Paige knows me just as well as I know her.

He merely commented, "If you say so."

Paige turned and looked at her former lover, and now friend. Her eyes narrowed, and pink lips pursed. But she said nothing more.

Stephen then added with satisfaction, "I like making you feel uncomfortable now and then."

"You try..." – Paige glanced around, smiled, and whispered – "lover."

Paige used to call Stephen that when they were together, and enjoyed reverting back to it on occasion for different reasons at different times.

And now I'm uncomfortable, which is exactly what Paige wanted.

Jennifer returned, and asked, "Did I miss anything?"

Before Stephen could answer, Paige said, "I apologize, Jennifer, but your husband was feeling a bit too comfortable, so I made him feel awkward."

Jennifer said, "I'm sorry I missed it."

Paige declared, "Well, no matter what he does or doesn't tell you, just know that I didn't mean any of it. Taming my tongue remains a challenge."

"Agreed," said Stephen with a wry smile.

Chapter 4

Most mornings, Pastor Stephen Grant went for an early run. This was part of his routine to keep his six-foot tall body in shape. On this Wednesday, the setting was far from typical for the black-haired, green-eyed Grant, with the Pacific Ocean on one side of him. Plus, on the other side was a running partner – Phil Lucena.

Jennifer and Stephen were guests at Phil and Jessica's place in Santa Cruz. Sean and Rachel McEnany would be staying there as well when they arrived later that night. Phil was playing overnight host, with Jessica staying at Melissa Ambler's.

The soon-to-be-married couple's modern-style beach house was on West Cliff Drive just a few miles west of the restaurant at which they all had enjoyed dinner the previous evening. The deep, narrow, light blue home featured a carport, storage space and large room used as a gym on the ground floor, with the second floor offering a deck above the parked cars. There were two staircases – one outside up to the deck and another in the house. The second floor featured an open space covering a living room, dining area and kitchen. The space had a peaked roof and large windows looking out on the water. Off the hallway running down the center of the back of the home were several rooms, including a master suite, three more bedrooms, and two bathrooms.

Of course, given what Phil and Jessica did for a living, the house had a state-of-the-art security system.

After jogging up the coast for about two miles and then back, the two men were easing down from their run –

walking on the path across the road from the house, and looking out at the ocean waters.

Grant didn't mind a partner, but he found it hard to talk while running. So, the two now were able to chat.

Grant asked, "Are you all set for the big event?"

Lucena nodded. "I am. Honestly, I kind of wonder what she's doing with me. I feel lucky."

Grant replied, "I think the same thing with Jennifer at times. I definitely married up."

Lucena smiled, "I get that."

"At the same time, neither person in a marriage is perfect, and thinking otherwise often doesn't bode well for when we all inevitably fall short."

"What are you trying to tell me about Jessica, Pastor?"

Grant recognized that Lucena was ribbing him. He continued, "Among the keys are understanding the other person, loving them even on those occasions when they're perhaps not all that loveable, being willing to both take responsibility and to forgive, and having something deep in common." He paused, and added, "Sorry. I slipped into pastor mode."

Lucena said, "I understand. And I want to thank you for helping Jess and me return to our faith, and recognizing how essential that is for our marriage."

"Whatever I might have contributed has been thanks to the Holy Spirit."

Lucena smiled, and said, "Yes, but you've got a job to do, and you do it well."

"Thanks."

"You're welcome. And now I think we need to get ready to head to the Sandcastle. We're meeting everyone there, and it's supposed to be about breakfast, and giving you and Jennifer a tour."

"Sounds good. I'm looking forward to it."

*   *   *

The CDM building, or the Sandcastle, in Santa Cruz had been a clandestine facility that CDM more or less inherited from the CIA. At the time, there had been little noteworthy about it from the outside, fitting comfortably into its commercial surroundings on River Street.

CDM recently enlarged the property in the back, purchasing a parking lot and retail store. Those were removed, and the one-story building extensively renovated, with parking shifted and expanded on the side of the facility. A wrought iron fence was replaced by a stucco-style 8 foot wall and massive, thick hedges that reached four feet higher than the wall. Neighbors and those passing by couldn't see in at all, and the driveway at the gated entrance turned sharply behind the hedges. After that quick turn, everything on the inside of the property opened up, with the driveway turning back into a parking area.

Lucena was behind the wheel of a small, white SUV, with Stephen Grant in the front passenger seat and Jennifer in the back seat.

Lucena turned the vehicle from River Street into the Sandcastle's driveway. He waited.

Stephen spotted the various security cameras, though he thought that few people with untrained eyes would notice them. They were small, and blended in nicely with the gate, wall and hedges.

After a few seconds, the gate opened.

As Lucena gently pressed down on the accelerator, he explained, "Facial recognition and a scan of the vehicle. If everything checks out, whoever is inside is given a greenlight. That person – it's more often than not Due, of course – does another check via cameras, etc., and then either opens the gate or raises questions."

Jennifer asked, "And Due lives here?"

"He does. Jessica and I did before we bought the house."

Lucena parked the SUV, and the three got out. Jennifer and Stephen looked beyond the back of the rather bland-looking building at what amounted to a large yard, with thick green grass, trees offering shade, a brick walkway, barbeque, a fire pit, and plenty of chairs and benches.

Stephen observed, "It comes across as a commercial business with a nice outdoor area for employees."

Jennifer added, "That's what I was thinking."

Lucena looked around, and replied, "Well, that's sort of what it is. Except the yard is for more than just lunch breaks." He looked directly at Stephen. "You've never been here before, right?"

"Right."

"This place always has been rather remarkable, but the build out that we've done was a major undertaking."

The three walked around the outside. Stephen noticed that there were only a few windows on the back portion – the new part – of the building, and they were high and small. He also noted more small, unobtrusive cameras.

As they came around to the front entrance and approached a thick metal door, Stephen asked, "I know this is a stupid question, but can you get onto the property or into the building without someone letting you in?"

Lucena chuckled. "Sure. Otherwise, Due could never leave. There are additional security steps before the gate and this door unlock. It takes longer."

Jennifer commented, "And I guess you hope that the ice cream you just picked up at the grocery store doesn't melt."

Lucena said, "That's actually true. Jess and I learned that the hard way."

The door clicked open. They stepped into a small room, and the front door closed behind them. Stephen felt uncomfortable as he looked around the tiny space. Another door was in front of them, but to their left and right, there were two ports. These could be slid open and closed from the other side of the wall. For good measure, there were two round and capped ports just above the floor.

Steel walls. This is a kill box meant for any unwanted visitors who somehow might have made it this far. Gun ports. The capped holes near the floor? Fire?

The hairs on his neck stood up.

The door in front of them opened, and a smiling Due Tran was standing there. "Welcome!"

Jennifer and Stephen greeted Tran, and the rest of the CDM group staying at the Sandcastle. And that was everyone who had been on their plane trip – Chase Axelrod,

Brooke Semmler, Kent Holtwick, Ellen Bracken, and Jordan Hall, as well as Paige Caldwell and Charlie Driessen.

Jessica West was already there as well, waiting for Lucena.

Jennifer asked, "You're all staying here? How big is this place?"

The slender, black-haired Due Tran smiled broadly, and said, "I'm so glad you asked. It's time for the tour." He turned and looked at Stephen, adding, "And since you're an unofficial employee, you guys get the full tour."

"Does anyone in this business now not refer to me as an unpaid, unofficial employee?" The joke had started between Stephen, Paige and Charlie, along with Sean McEnany, but had now spread to the entire CDM staff.

Driessen chuckled, and commented, "What else do you want, Grant, an 'Employee of the Month' certificate when you help out?"

"That at least might be nice."

"Oh, stop your whining," said Caldwell.

Tran then took over and started the tour. "With the expansion, we rearranged a great deal."

While nondescript at best on the outside, the inside of the Sandcastle verged on luxurious, with assorted comforts and cutting-edge technology.

After emerging from what Grant referred to as a "kill box" in his head, they stood in a wide hallway. A door on the right led into an arsenal, with wall units stocking handguns, shotguns, submachine guns, machine guns, bullet proof vests, night-vision goggles, assorted grenades – gas and otherwise, Stephen noted – and tactical knives.

He also noted a unit with a screen and assorted controls built into the wall on the other side of the small entry area. Stephen pointed and asked, "Is that for the 'kill box'?"

Tran hesitated and then answered, "We don't call it that, but yes."

What do you call it?

The door on the other side of the hallway opened into the communications center. Stephen was duly impressed. In the center of the room was a large computer table showing a map of the Pacific Rim. And two large video screens hung on the wall to the right of the doorway. Along the walls to the left and across the room were long tables with two desktop computers on each, and a printer-scanner on each as well. Leather office chairs populated the room, along with a small couch to the immediate right of the door and a large, plush recliner to the left. The recliner seemed out of place to Stephen, but he reflected that if a situation called for an extended period of time in this room, that probably was appreciated.

Stepping beyond the hallway, they came into a massive, wide open room that featured three main areas – a library to the right, a kitchen to the left, and across the back, a sprawling living room.

The library featured bookcases against the wall, and four-foot bookcases provided a dividing line with the living room. There was a small couch, an armchair, tables with lamps, and a coffee table in the center.

The kitchen was commercial-quality, with all stainless-steel appliances, and a center island with high-backed stools. There also was a long dining table that rested between the kitchen and living room.

As for the living room, a huge flat-screen television hung on one wall, in front of a half-circle of seating – four reclining, theater style seats, a couch, and a rocking recliner. Beyond that section was sprinkled more seating, a pinball machine, and a bar with stools.

Tran stopped in front of a group of wall-hangings featuring the San Francisco Giants.

Stephen asked, "A Giants fan, Due?"

"I've become one in honor of Zhu Gao. He loved baseball and the Giants. And since I arrived and came to hear about his work, I've followed his lead."

"I like that," replied Stephen.

Zhu Gao had set up this building for the CIA. He had worked for the Chinese Ministry of State Security, but after witnessing the atrocities of Tiananmen Square, he turned. Gao wound up spying on the communist Chinese government, and eventually escaped China with CIA help, including from Stephen Grant, Paige Caldwell and Charlie Driessen. Later, Gao lost his life when he and Driessen were attacked.

What made this open space unique was a ceiling that let in natural light during the day and views of the stars at night. Adjustments could be made to vary how much light was allowed into the building, while this was all undetectable from the outside. No ability existed to see inside. From above, the roof had the look of solar panels, while the material was shatterproof, having the strength of steel.

Tran also noted that the rest of the building was built with layers, including cinderblocks on the outside, steel, and eventually on the inside, a kind of sheetrock. Tran pointed out, "No one outside can hear what's happening in here."

Jennifer's question as to where everyone stayed was then answered. There were a total of seven bedroom suites – three directly off the living room, and four more down a hallway. The bedrooms either offered a king-sized bed or two queens, and an accompanying bathroom featuring a walk-in shower and a separate Jacuzzi tub.

Finally, a basement included not just a storage area, but an extensively equipped gym and a shooting range.

After the tour, Stephen said to Caldwell and Driessen, "Well, you guys don't skimp with your offices in Virginia or with this."

Caldwell said, "We're global, and we have the best people. We want to keep them happy, properly taken care of and correctly equipped."

Jennifer observed, "You've definitely achieved that. I'd love to see what's up in the Virginia office."

Caldwell said, "Next time you're in D.C., let's arrange for you to come over. We'll have lunch or dinner, and talk about Stephen when he's not around."

The two women smiled, and looked at Stephen.

Driessen glanced over and said to Stephen, "You're screwed."

The entire group gathered in and around the kitchen for breakfast.

After breakfast was finished and all traces of the meal cleaned up, people started to wander away for various undertakings and duties.

That included Stephen, Jessica and Phil heading over to Trinity Lutheran Church to meet with Pastor Orel Gibson. It would be the final meet-up of their pre-marital counseling sessions, and Stephen was glad that he would be there in person, rather than over a video chat, this time.

As for Jennifer, she asked Tran, "I have some work to do, but rather than heading back to Phil and Jessica's, would you mind if I set up my laptop here?"

"Of course, I don't mind. That would be wonderful."

As Stephen went to leave, he asked Jennifer, "You're all set then?"

"Stephen, are you kidding? It's hard to think of a better place to work."

They would all reassemble later that evening, being joined by Sean and Rachel McEnany, for a casual wine-and-cheese gathering at the home of Jessica and Phil.

Chapter 5

The dark brown shingles of Trinity Lutheran Church had a weathered but warm look. That wasn't surprising. The building sat atop a hill. And though the water was a little over a mile-and-a-half away, a clear view was offered of the Pacific Ocean from the church's front door. That also meant that the salty ocean breezes could be felt, along with the warmth of the California sun.

Phil Lucena and Jessica West led Pastor Stephen Grant to the top of the front steps, where they stopped and turned. Grant followed their lead.

Oh, nice.

The sunlight glistened on the blue water. Given the size of the Pacific, it seemed much closer than the actual distance.

"That's simply awesome," Grant commented.

West replied, "I know. And that spot over there" – she was pointing to a raised, flat stone and grass area to the left – "is great for pictures. It captures the view perfectly."

As Grant was taking in the scenery, the door opened behind him.

Grant turned to see Pastor Orel Gibson. Trinity's pastor declared, "If you think this is nice, sunset is breathtaking. It never gets old." Gibson was tall and thick, with short blond hair coupled with a bushy beard. Nonetheless, a wide smile could be seen through the facial hair. "Welcome, Stephen."

As the two men shook hands, Grant replied, "It's good to see you in the flesh, Orel, rather than on a computer screen."

"It is."

Gibson greeted West and Lucena, and invited the three inside. After a tour of the building, they settled into a conference room.

Grant looked for a cue from his fellow pastor.

Gibson said, "This is your wedding – I mean, it's their wedding, but you're officiating. As I said before, I'm an assistant and a host. You've led the last three pre-marriage classes from a distance, and now you're here, in person, to do this last one."

Grant said, "Thanks, but I'm a guest. This is your church, and the home church for you two" – he looked at West and Lucena.

Lucena said, "Thanks to you, Stephen."

Grant smiled in response, and looked specifically at West and Lucena. "So, do you two have any questions about what we've covered, including the readings?"

Lucena glanced at West, and she said, "About that 'submit' thing..." And then she laughed. "I'm sorry, but I couldn't resist. And I have no doubt you get this all of the time, so, I figured, 'Why not ask?'"

She glanced at Lucena, who was smiling seemingly in slight discomfort.

Grant chuckled. "Yeah, I get this question a lot, as I'm sure Pastor Gibson does."

Gibson replied, "Naturally," with a smile once more evident behind the beard.

Grant continued, "And you're right, of course, 'Why not ask?' Let's quickly review what St. Paul writes in Ephesians 5. We'll pick it up at verse 20."

Grant found the right place in the Bible and read:

> [G]iving thanks always and for everything to God the Father in the name of our Lord Jesus Christ, submitting to one another out of reverence for Christ.
>
> Wives, submit to your own husbands, as to the Lord. For the husband is the head of the wife even as Christ is the head of the church, his body, and is himself its Savior. Now as the

church submits to Christ, so also wives should submit in everything to their husbands.

Husbands, love your wives, as Christ loved the church and gave himself up for her, that he might sanctify her, having cleansed her by the washing of water with the word, so that he might present the church to himself in splendor, without spot or wrinkle or any such thing, that she might be holy and without blemish. In the same way husbands should love their wives as their own bodies. He who loves his wife loves himself. For no one ever hated his own flesh, but nourishes and cherishes it, just as Christ does the church, because we are members of his body. "Therefore a man shall leave his father and mother and hold fast to his wife, and the two shall become one flesh." This mystery is profound, and I am saying that it refers to Christ and the church. However, let each one of you love his wife as himself, and let the wife see that she respects her husband.

Grant looked around the table. "Today, that phrase about wives submitting to their husbands jumps out at people. You know what jumps out at me, though?"

Lucena shook his head, while West shrugged.

Grant continued, "It's when Paul says this is a profound mystery, notes that he's referring to Christ and the Church, and finishes up by basically saying that men should love their wives, and women should respect their husbands. Sometimes, I get the feeling that he's wrapping things up and trying to move on."

That drew a laugh from Pastor Gibson.

West and Lucena tittered as well, with West then asking, "Is that, in fact, it?"

Grant said, "No. I'm just joking to get us perhaps thinking a little differently than we normally might. St. Paul is inviting the married couple to be an image, if you will, that points us toward the relationship between Christ and His Church, that the love between husband and wife leads us to a conversation about God's divine love, which brings us back around to understanding the marriage relationship. Don't get too caught up in that word 'submit,' but understand that it's being applied to all of us – that we each submit to other Christians for the sake of Christ, submit to the Lord, and the Church submits to Christ. It isn't the culture that informs the deep meaning of the word 'submit' here, but instead, Christ and his relationship to the Church that does so. That leads us to think about how Christ treats the Church, and how the Church responds. When Paul talks of how Christ treats the Church, it's quite profound and moving, and in turn, he is calling on husbands to be Christ-like to their wives, and quite frankly vice versa. This isn't some tyrannical decree, allowing husbands to control and do as they like to their spouses. Quite the contrary, this is about sacrificial love, all-forgiving, even unconditional love. Think about what Paul says – 'Husbands, love your wives, as Christ loved the church and gave himself up for her.' He is talking about Christ dying for the Church, for each of us. And what happens when a spouse inevitably fails in being Christ-like in marriage – after all, we're all sinners – when we rebel against God's Word? We forgive and love, again unconditionally, just like Christ. We do all of this, by the way, by submitting to our Lord."

West said, "That's a different way of looking at this passage, to say the least."

After some further discussion, Grant asked, "Other questions?"

Lucena said, "If I may, I admit that I was, at first, kind of surprised that you had us read an article from *The New York Times* titled 'Why You Will Marry the Wrong Person.' But after reading it, we both" – he glanced at West who nodded – "saw the wisdom, namely, that despite the prevailing views of what marriage is supposed to be about, no one is perfect – neither your spouse nor you – and we will, at various times and probably more often than presumed at the start of our marriage, annoy and disappoint each other. In part, that's due to the unattainable ideal established that the other person will meet all our needs and yearnings."

West added, "I liked the point made by the author – Alain de Botton, right? Yes – that compatibility is achieved via love, and that includes forgiveness, rather than being a precondition of love. I simply never thought of it that way."

Grant said, "It's a short essay, but it hits home."

"Is he a Christian?" asked Lucena.

Grant shook his head. "He's an atheist. And I think that makes this article even more powerful. After all, he's certainly hitting on Christian points about marriage, given the sinful aspects of human nature, Christ's forgiveness and our call to forgive."

A bit later in the conversation, Grant asked Gibson, "Anything to add, Orel?"

Pastor Gibson looked at West and Lucena, and said, "To follow up on Stephen's points, you never know what's going to happen in life, and that means the pledge you make – to each other, before God as well as before your family and friends, to love, sacrifice for, serve and forgive each other no matter what comes – is, indeed, Christ-like, in that Jesus loves, has sacrificed for, serves and forgives each of us. That's a radical, very public declaration about your marriage and marriage in general."

When their discussion came to an end and each rose from the table, Grant said, "Let's head into the sanctuary and we'll do a quick review of how the service will proceed."

Lucena, West and Gibson agreed, with Gibson adding, "Of course, we'll walk through everything on Friday evening as well with the entire bridal party, and then off to the rehearsal dinner."

Chapter 6

After nearly four decades with the CIA, Jeff Oakes had retired a couple of years ago to a small coastal town in Maine called Clement Point.

He appreciated the relaxed pace, the people, and the cold, including the coolness of the summers. And he particularly enjoyed the views from his front porch of the rocky coast line, looking down on the actual Clement Point jetting out into the waters of the Atlantic Ocean, the village and its harbor, and three islands not too far in the distance.

While conversation, wine and cheese were wrapping up at the home of Jessica West and Phil Lucena on the Pacific Ocean, Oakes slept with the bedroom window opened slightly to let in some chilly October air and sounds of the Atlantic.

That ajar window also let in other noises.

Oakes' home was the only house at the end of a short, narrow road.

A black minivan with its lights off turned onto the street, and parked behind trees short of the sightlines from the house.

Three men exited the vehicle. Each was dressed in black from head to toe, and carried a Sig Sauer P365 with a suppresser attached.

They moved quickly and quietly toward the home, and fanned out. While doing so, one of the assassins stepped on and cracked a small branch. It didn't seem to make much noise, and the man kept moving. But in the second floor bedroom, Oakes' eyes popped open.

One of the assailants swung off a small backpack, and pulled out a targeted EMP device. He triggered it, and power was lost throughout the home.

With a Beretta M9 pistol now in hand, Oakes stood motionless – listening – inside the doorway of his bedroom.

The front and back doors of the home made the slightest noises as they were opened.

Two assailants moved stealthily around the first floor in search of their prey.

Oakes looked at the glass door leading to the second floor deck outside his bedroom. He remained unmoving. He waited. Once he heard the slight creaks as the intruders stepped onto the staircase, Oakes moved to the door, opened it and stepped out onto the deck.

He quietly closed the door behind him, and started for the rope stored inside a box. Oakes kept it there in case he had to lower himself to the ground due to a fire in the home, or if he somehow had unexpected visitors, whether common criminals or people from his past.

But as he began to reach down, a voice came from behind. "Let's not do that, mate."

Oakes whirled and began to raise his Beretta. But it was too late.

The assassin pulled the trigger three times, and each shot found its target.

Oakes fell back against the gray siding of the home, and slid down to the deck. His body was in a sitting position, leaning against the box with his escape rope.

The killer walked over, picked up Oakes' gun, and tossed it off the deck.

Through the black mask, the man said, "Bloody hell, we're not stupid enough to have all of us inside the house. Other than shooting it out, this was your most obvious play."

With blood leaking from two bullet wounds in his chest, and one in his stomach, Oakes couldn't move. The arrival of death was inevitable. He managed to ask, "Why?"

All his murderer said was, "Orders rooted in revenge."

The assailant moved by Oakes, and met his two comrades in the house. In turn, they left as quietly as they came.

Minutes crept by, and Oakes struggled to write something on the decking using a finger and his own blood.

Eventually, minutes became more than three hours. Oakes' breathing grew more labored. His weakness spread.

As the sun began to rise, the dark sky turned a mix of blue and yellow. Finally, the sun began to peek over the waters of the Atlantic. Oakes' eyes were transfixed on the growing illumination. He managed to smile ever so slightly, and then he gave up his last breath.

By mid-morning, his slumped body was spotted from the road by a jogger.

Not long after that, Clement Point Police Chief Sutton Knight stood next to one of her two deputies, looking down at Jeff Oakes' body and the message he scrawled.

The deputy squinted his eyes as if that would help clarify the message in blood. "Brit?"

Knight replied, "Yes. And it looks like the second word might have been 'revenge,' but he ran out of strength or time, just managing to get to an 'n.'"

"I'd agree, ma'am."

Knight looked at her deputy, and provided the reminder that she had for nearly every day since taking the job. "Let's stick with 'chief,' and not 'ma'am.'"

The deputy winced. "Right. Right. Sorry."

"It's okay. Mr. Oakes was former CIA, so when I get back to the office, I'll give them a ring and see if they can shed some light on this."

Chapter 7

Thursday was marked for Jessica West's bachelorette party, and Phil Lucena's bachelor party. Other than letting invitees know the time, the matron of honor – Melissa Ambler – and the best man – Charlie Driessen – had kept the details secret until the night before.

Everyone received texts on Wednesday night with the details. As Jennifer reviewed them in bed next to Stephen, she commented, "I think the phrase capturing Jessica's party would be 'lavish but low key.'"

"And Phil's?" asked Stephen.

"A guys' night, but more mature than most bachelor parties."

"I'm not sure who's getting the better day – the ladies or the guys?"

"I'm pretty sure that each group will be pleased, but if you can't see that we ladies are getting the better night overall, then I have serious questions about you, dear husband."

"Really? Tell me that there's not some small part of you that would prefer doing what the men are."

She shrugged slightly, and said, "Maybe. A little."

Stephen's chuckle was a tad extended.

"What else are you laughing at?" asked Jennifer.

"Charlie Driessen caught up in planning any part of a wedding is more than amusing." He looked down at the details on his phone. "Then again, I'm guessing he had help."

"Paige?"

"Most likely."

"Either way, I didn't realize that Phil and Charlie were so close that Charlie is his best man."

"Yeah, neither one is exactly chatty. But they've been through a lot together."

"Do you mind if I ask a question about Jessica?"

"What is it?"

"I haven't seen or heard much talk about her family? And she only has Melissa and Paige in the wedding party."

"I know. She's had a tough time, as you know, with the death of her father in Afghanistan, and her brother in Iraq. And then her first fiancé, who worked with her at the FBI, died in the New York bombing."

Jennifer shook her head slowly. "Dear Lord, she's been through so much."

Stephen continued, "So, as far as I'm aware, there will be some relatives at the wedding, but it doesn't seem like she's very close to them."

They sat in silence for a few minutes, and then Stephen added, "There's a rare, complementary aspect to their relationship that didn't need to develop. I think it was just there from the start. Phil is a kind of steadying rock for Jessica, which has allowed a certain openness or lightness to emerge, or apparently re-emerge. It provides some needed balance to the harshness she holds in reaction to the deaths of her father, brother and first fiancé. In turn, I think that lightness has been good for Phil."

"How so?"

"It's just an impression, but his unrelenting politeness seems to be about more than just how he was raised. I think it has worked for him in maintaining some distance from others. You mentioned the wedding party; it's a similar story for the guys – only Charlie and Chase."

She nodded. "Yeah. It's all very CDM – especially given how Jessica and Melissa met."

"Right. For Jessica and Melissa, I'm sure it's not just beach volleyball, but also the fact that they've each suffered such terrible losses."

Jennifer nodded.

"On the positive side," Stephen continued, "all of this speaks well of how close that entire group is, and it's not surprising given how deeply they rely on each other."

Stephen turned, looked at Jennifer, and added, "You know, Jessica helps Phil like you've helped me."

Stephen leaned over and kissed her.

Jennifer then smiled, and said, "Okay, fair enough, and you've done your part for me, similar to what Phil does for Jessica." She paused, and then added, "On a completely different note, I've long thought that Melissa and Jessica are two of the most beautiful women I've ever met – tall, in seemingly perfect shape, blond hair, blue eyes – and quite frankly, they look like they could be sisters. And on top of it all, they play beach volleyball."

Stephen smirked, and said, "I'm not sure how to respond to that without the possibility of getting in trouble."

"That means you agree with me, but you're being a jerk."

"Guilty. But let me add, that neither Jessica nor Melissa approach your beauty. You're the prettiest gal I know."

Jennifer raised an eyebrow and smiled. "Good answer. But 'the prettiest gal' you know? Golly, gee, what year is this? Too many old movies for you."

* * *

The Lodge at Pebble Beach not only offered a famous golf course and breathtaking vistas of Monterey Bay, but its other experiences ranked as world class.

The first stop was The Inn at Spanish Bay. Eight women exited an extra-long limousine on mid-Thursday afternoon. The group reflected what Stephen and Jennifer had been talking about in terms of the circle of people closest to Jessica West. In addition to Jessica, Melissa Ambler and Jennifer Grant, the bachelorette party was completed by Paige Caldwell, Rachel McEnany, Brooke Semmler, Ellen Bracken and Jordan Hall.

As a member of Pebble and the related properties, Ambler had arranged the festivities for the late afternoon and far into the evening.

A swim at Spanish Bay's surfside pool kicked things off. Drinks and light hors d'oeuvres were served poolside.

After nearly two hours of relaxation and conversation, Ambler asked the group, "Are you ready to use the spa treatment, ladies?"

After they changed, the limo driver took the portion of 17-Mile Drive that journeyed south along the surf from the inn to The Spa at Pebble Beach. The spa services normally ended at 5:00 p.m., and it was now nearly six. But Ambler had arranged for a special session.

Each guest could choose among the various spa scrubs – a Papaya Pineapple Scrub, Sea Salt Scrub, Café Menthe Scrub, or Wild Rose Scrub – followed by a classic Swedish massage.

Jennifer and Paige wound up on tables next to each other in one of the massage suites.

Paige commented, "This is incredible."

Jennifer smiled. "I couldn't agree more." A few seconds passed, and she continued, "By the way, Stephen and I were talking last night about Charlie being Phil's best man, and..."

Paige interrupted, "Yeah, I made the arrangements for the bachelor party. And I mean *all* of the arrangements."

Jennifer laughed. "We thought so."

"Please. The idea of Charlie being involved in planning anything related to a wedding is simply absurd."

A few minutes later, Paige observed, "You and I getting massages next to each other will make Stephen very uncomfortable."

"Oh, I'm well aware."

"I trust you'll use it to bother him."

"Count on it."

They both laughed.

Jennifer added, "Of course, it tends to work best when we do that together."

Paige smiled. "It is. We'll have to look for an opportunity to drop it on him over the next few days."

"We can enjoy it even if he doesn't."

Paige responded, "I'm so glad he married you."

Everyone reconvened by another pool – the spa's outdoor pool in which the water was set to 82 degrees.

Jennifer eventually made her way into the waters for a swim. She emerged from under the water, and found herself at one end of the pool with Ambler, West and Brooke Semmler. Jennifer pulled her auburn hair back from her face, and smiled at her three friends. "Is this for the beach volleyball set only?"

Semmler had played briefly with West on a CDM assignment. She, too, was athletic and had blue eyes, with light brown hair. She replied, "These two are the pros."

West responded, "Don't sell yourself short, Brooke."

Ambler agreed with West. "Yeah, I've been after you to try out for our tour."

Jennifer eventually shifted gears, reflecting, "This has been a fantastic day."

West responded, "It has." She gazed across the three faces looking at her, adding, "Thank you, so much."

Jennifer quickly said, "This was all Melissa. She wouldn't take any help." Semmler echoed that comment.

West said, "I figured. Thanks, Mel, and Jennifer and Brooke, thank you for making the trip."

"I never would have missed you and Phil getting married," Jennifer replied, "even if Stephen wasn't doing the service."

Semmler chimed in, "And how could I miss the wedding of my onetime volleyball partner?"

They spoke a bit more about the wedding, and then Ambler said, "Have I mentioned how happy I am for you and Phil?"

"Of course, you have," answered West.

The two exchanged a hug, and Ambler then wiped either a tear or pool water away from the corner of an eye. She turned to Jennifer and Brooke, "The day is far from over. We're going to have a private dinner party on the second floor of the Lodge. It has a fantastic view of the bay. And after dinner, it's the Lodge's specialty drinks and live music."

*	*	*

The bachelor party involved another limousine, but the journey was farther. The agenda for Phil Lucena, Charlie Driessen, Stephen Grant, Chase Axelrod, Due Tran, Sean McEnany, and Kent Holtwick was dinner atop the Hyatt Place Hotel at the KAIYO Rooftop restaurant in San Francisco. That would be followed by taking in a Giants playoff game.

While enjoying the view and the food at the restaurant, the conversation varied widely from the upcoming game and the overall postseason to post-wedding plans for Lucena and West to general ribbing. During the short walk to the ballpark, the good-natured jabs continued.

Grant said, "Your knowledge of great Asian fusion spots in San Francisco was revelatory, Charlie."

McEnany added, "I had no clue, either. What else are you hiding, Charlie?"

"Yeah, yeah, cut the bullshit. Paige made the dinner arrangements, and Due got the Giants tickets."

McEnany commented, "I'm just shocked. And it makes me wonder, what exactly are you doing as best man anyway?"

Grant looked over at Lucena, and asked, "Phil, are you trusting him with the rings, or has someone else got that covered, too?"

Driessen said, "Some people might have a problem telling a pastor to screw off, but I'm not one of those people."

Grant and the others laughed.

After passing by the Juan Marichal statue – with the pitching great portrayed doing his patented high leg kick windup – the group entered the ballpark through the Lefty O'Doul gate.

Grant had never been inside the Giants ballpark before, and he, along with the rest of the party, enjoyed the game. But Grant particularly appreciated sitting next to Tran, as the two discussed the various features of the stadium, including the field's unique dimensions, the large Coca-Cola bottle and old-time glove looming over the left field bleachers, and the view they had from their seats of the waters of McCovey Cove beyond right field. A home run wound up splashing down in the cove, with kayakers scrambling to recover the ball. That dinger put the Giants ahead for good – again, to the particular delight of Due Tran.

Chapter 8

Victoria Wilsey knew the meaning of the word "patience" – waiting years to take revenge for the death of her husband, Bertram.

But the time hadn't been wasted. Using the resources she and her late spouse had accumulated by ranking among the world's leading and most mysterious arms dealers, Wilsey built a well-respected business specializing in cutting-edge body armor for British soldiers, as well as a recent expansion to European allies. The United States was proving a tougher nut to crack. But she now had spent much of the past year partnering with a California firm to gain a foothold with the U.S. military.

At the same time, she never abandoned arms dealing with some of the world's worst regimes and terrorists.

When speaking to her son, Adlai, with no one else present, Victoria relished referring to the two enterprises as producing "a not-so-virtuous cycle," whereby she sold weapons to terrorists and rogue regimes, and armor to protect those targeted by such evildoers. Her son seemed enamored with all of his mother's actions and comments.

As arms dealers, Victoria and Bertram had used every possible safeguard – including setting up two very different lives, one public and one deep in the shadows – to ensure that whomever in their organization might be killed or captured, tracks would never lead all the way back to the source, to those in command. And after Bertram's death, Victoria took the public life, and turned it into leadership of a formidable business, which earned her the respect of many, including in the British government.

Victoria also presented intimidating mannerisms and looks. Her short black hair, arched eyebrows, sharp nose and pointed chin created a forbidding face, and that rested atop a thin frame. Her voice exuded confidence, as did her surprisingly strong grip when shaking hands.

Through a close contact in MI-6, Victoria managed to acquire the CIA file that told the details of Bertram's death on a frigid night on the fortress island of Suomenlinna – the "Castle of Finland" – at the entrance of Helsinki's South Harbor. She knew where, when and how he had died, but not the people who had committed the act. The file provided that information.

After waiting years to acquire the information, she still exhibited exceptional patience. Victoria sought just the right moment, and that was now here.

Her sprawling adobe-style home was perched far above Avalon and its harbor, all located on Santa Catalina Island. The tiny town featured palm trees; the Green Pleasure Pier; sand; and the white, 12-story, round, Art Deco Catalina Island Casino theater. The island was located some 22 miles offshore from Los Angeles.

While Jessica West and Phil Lucena were celebrating their bachelorette and bachelor parties up the coast, Victoria Wilsey was going over the plans she had for both, as well as for Charlie Driessen. As her team was gathered on an expansive rooftop patio, the harbor lights of Avalon, including on the pier and theater, glowed and flickered, and reflected on the water.

Wilsey declared, "Excellent work was done with Oakes in Maine, and now, the time is here to strike while these people are gathered together in California." She proceeded to review the plan, once again, with the 21 men who made up her personal security force, along with her two personal bodyguards and her son. The assault would start at the home of Phil Lucena. "Team A will strike fast and hard, and if possible, make sure that Lucena's fiancée dies before he does, and that he knows it, even sees it occur, before you end him." Several of the mercenaries nodded in approval. Wilsey continued, "As word, no doubt, gets back to the CDM building, they will move to assist, and when they emerge from the property, Team B will strike." A few more points were reviewed, and she asked, "Does anyone have questions?"

One man stepped forward.

"Yes?" responded Wilsey.

"As you know, that place in Santa Cruz is quite the fortification. Are we sure that the first attack will draw them all out?"

Wilsey smiled. "Come, come now. You know that there are no guarantees. Worst case scenario, we complete the job at the house, and live to try another day. Best case, they react to word about the house attack, and then we have our opportunity. In that case, perhaps one or two stay behind for some reason. Again, another day's opportunity." She paused and then said, "But from what we've seen and understand, the chances that Driessen will remain inside the building are slim."

After a few more questions were answered, Wilsey added, "There are multiple benefits to be had by our actions. Not only will long overdue retaliation be executed, but the elimination of this CDM firm will be a plus by removing an ongoing threat to our business and a message will be sent to the CIA. Each of you will be rewarded beyond what already has been provided in terms of compensation."

The team leader, Jason Cox, replied, "You've already been tremendously generous, Mrs. Wilsey. We appreciate it, and we will not fail you."

His 20 team members voiced their approval. "Hear, hear."

Wilsey smiled, particularly at Cox, and said, "Thank you, gentlemen."

Adlai raised an eyebrow at his mother's glance at Cox.

She then looked at the sun setting on the Pacific, turned to her guests and announced, "Please enjoy the drinks and more food is coming."

It all had an air of civility, even grace and beauty, given the location.

Chapter 9

The rehearsal dinner on Friday night took place at a small Italian restaurant less than a half-mile from the beach. Jennifer sat on one side of Stephen Grant, and Charlie Driessen on the other.

As dessert – a choice of frozen chocolate-chip meringata or cherries poached in red wine with Mascarpone Cream – was being served, Driessen leaned over to Stephen, and whispered, "Don't tell anyone, but I'm actually enjoying these few days."

Stephen smiled. "Glad to hear it. Your secret is safe with me."

"There is something to the idea of being able to relax in California."

"You've grown so much, Charlie," commented Stephen.

Driessen leaned closer and looked at Jennifer. She moved her head in tighter to Stephen as well. And in this small huddle, Driessen looked at Jennifer and said, "Sometimes your husband is a bit of an asshole."

Jennifer laughed, and Stephen raised an eyebrow at her. She replied, "Well, Charlie has known you longer than I have, so who am I to argue?"

It was Driessen's turn to chuckle, and he replied, "You really are his better half."

Just then Driessen's smartphone rumbled in his pocket. He pulled it out and looked at the screen. "Shit. So much for relaxing. Give me a minute."

Stephen and Jennifer nodded, and each dug into the desserts.

Several minutes later, Stephen watched Driessen return and whisper in Paige Caldwell's ear. Others at the table were watching as well. As Caldwell rose from her chair, she looked at Sean McEnany and then at Phil Lucena.

As the four exited the room reserved for the party, Stephen's impulse was to follow. He looked at Jennifer. She whispered, "Find out if everything is okay."

Stephen stepped into the cool, salt air, and walked over to the group of four. "Mind if I eavesdrop?"

Caldwell said, "Of course not."

Driessen said, "I just told them that I received word from Tank that Jeff Oakes was killed earlier this week. Murdered. Professional hit."

Edward "Tank" Hoard had worked with each person standing in a circle outside the Italian restaurant while they were at the CIA. Hoard had remained at the Agency and now was director of the National Clandestine Service.

Grant didn't really know Oakes, but had spoken to him a few times during his stint with the CIA. "Dear God. What happened?"

"Yeah, I was just getting to that. Oakes had retired to a town in Maine, Clement Point, and the police chief there contacted the CIA because while he was dying, Jeff tried to spell out a message on the floor with his blood. The clear word was 'Brit.' But he only managed part of a second word. It looks like he was trying write 'revenge,' and got as far as the 'n.' Eventually, the message got to Tank."

Lucena continued, "And Tank is thinking about our encounter at Suomenlinna."

Caldwell and McEnany knew the story, but Grant didn't.

Seeing the look on Stephen's face, Lucena quickly brought him up to speed, including the British accents and the fact that none of those killed that night could subsequently be linked to any arms dealers.

Driessen continued, "Oakes had a long career, so I asked Tank if this could point to something else. He agreed that it could, and mentioned a couple of MI-6 related incidents that Oakes had been involved with as examples. But he wanted to let me know what happened, and that this *could* link back to Finland."

They stood in silence. Grant knew that each of the others were thinking the same thing he was.

Could be one of those other incidents. But we have to assume the worst possibility is in the mix, and it could extend to either Phil or Charlie. That doesn't mean changing anything scheduled for the wedding. But it does mean being on watch.

And that's exactly the conclusion that the five reached in conversation over the next few minutes.

"I'll let Jess know after the dinner."

Grant also knew that Jessica West would agree. After all, this is the life each person chose, including Grant, even though he was a pastor now.

The lone change of schedule that Phil insisted upon was that Jessica stay at their house on this pre-wedding night. Without providing the explicit details as to why, West told Melissa Ambler that she wouldn't be going back to Ambler's place.

Ambler said, "Don't worry. I'll bring all of your stuff over to your house in the morning."

They hugged, and Jessica said, "Thanks so much, for everything."

Three couples – Stephen and Jennifer, Sean and Rachel McEnany, and Jessica and Phil – journeyed back to Phil and Jessica's house.

Chapter 10

It was just past three in the morning when two black SUVs moved along West Cliff Drive. In the front passenger seat of the lead vehicle, Jason Cox spoke into a smartphone. "We're approaching the target." The call to the other team – Team B positioned outside CDM's Sandcastle – ended with that brief report.

The two vehicles pulled into the short driveway of the light blue beach house – blocking any possible exit from the home's carport.

Six men dressed in black streamed out of the lead vehicle, with five more emerging from the second SUV.

With Cox leading the way, the six went for the outside stairs leading up to the deck. The other five moved for the door into the lower part of the home.

*   *   *

With Jessica staying at the house, Phil Lucena was sleeping on the couch in the family room. When the first attacker outside stepped within a few feet of the carport, the camera alarm went off on his phone. Lucena rolled over, and with his eyes closed he found the phone on the coffee table. He opened his eyes, clicked on the security app, and bolted upright when the camera revealed figures dressed in black and holding weapons outside the house.

Lucena reached under the coffee table, and pulled a Glock 19 from a holster attached to the table's underside.

In the master bedroom, Jessica West had seen the same thing on her phone. With a Glock 20 in hand as she stepped into the hallway, the sound of the downstairs door crashing open came next. She looked beyond the kitchen and into the family room, spotting Lucena. She called out, "I've got the backstairs."

He nodded, and replied, "I have the front."

As Jessica moved down the hall, she rapped on the other two bedroom doors, and called out, "Get out here. We're under attack."

Sean McEnany's eyes already had opened at the sound of the alarm. He had installed the home's security system, and synced up his phone before going to sleep. When seeing the invaders, he had called Paige Caldwell, and said, "We're under attack, and might need help."

Caldwell's response was, "We're on our way. Stay safe."

Sean then moved his muscular, five-foot, ten-inch frame to the closet, and grabbed two Glocks from a case. Handing one to Rachel, who like her husband had once worked in national security and was no stranger to firearms, Sean asked, "Are you ready?"

While checking the weapon, Rachel took a deep breath and answered, "I am."

Jessica's call came, and the two stepped into the hallway. Across from them, Pastor Stephen Grant emerged from another bedroom. "I told Jen to stay put." He looked around.

McEnany said, "Go with Jessica and we'll cover things with Phil."

Grant nodded, and moved to his left, while Sean and Rachel went in the other direction.

Chapter 11

Within three minutes of getting the call from McEnany, Caldwell had spread the word throughout the Sandcastle.

Another two minutes, and Charlie Driessen, Chase Axelrod, Kent Holtwick, and Brooke Semmler had joined Caldwell in exiting the building, and piling into one of CDM's armored SUVs. Due Tran remained behind as a central point for communications, along with Ellen Bracken and Jordan Hall.

Driessen was behind the wheel, with Caldwell in the front passenger seat.

The gate to the CDM compound started to open.

*   *   *

Wilsey's Team B hid at various points along the street outside the CDM facility.

Two men were in a black car parked about 100 yards from the entrance. As the gate slid open, one said, "They're coming out." Each member of the strike team heard through an earpiece.

Driessen turned the SUV onto the street. His foot just started to press down harder on the accelerator when a rocket-propelled grenade came streaming at the vehicle. It struck the SUV's front grill and exploded.

Driessen instinctively turned the steering wheel, and a second grenade from another darkened position hit the side of the vehicle.

The force and position of the second explosion sent the SUV up onto two wheels. And then the vehicle fell on its side, and skidded to a stop.

Inside the Sandcastle, Tran, Bracken and Hall watched the events unfold on one of the screens.

Tran jumped to his feet, and said, "Please, stay here." He then ran to the armory by the front door.

On the street in front of the CDM property, the ten members of the assault team emerged from their various hiding places, and advanced toward the SUV.

Chapter 12

Stephen Grant arrived at the end of the hallway. He positioned himself next to West on the knob side of the closed door. He heard the ground level door crash open.

Grant decided to take the initiative. "You go low and I'll stay high."

"Good. On my count."

She crouched down low, and Grant moved closer to the door, now looming over West.

They listened as boots hit the stairs.

In a low voice, West said, "Three. Two. One."

She swung the door open, and dropped flat on the floor.

The two began firing.

Three intruders were advancing up the stairs, with two more scanning the downstairs and waiting for their opportunity to ascend as well. The attacker in front caught two projectiles and fell forward, now presenting an obstacle for the four men behind him. The second man in line took a projectile in the face and fell back. The third man caught him with his left arm, used his fallen comrade as a shield, and returned fire with an Uzi submachine gun.

West and Grant leaned back from the doorway, and shielded their eyes.

At a break in the firing, West stuck her head back out and looked down the staircase. She spotted the fourth man, who had just stepped onto the bottom step of the stairs, as he began to throw an object.

She yelled, "Grenade!"

Grant reached down, grabbed the back of West's shirt, and pulled her away as the grenade came through the doorway. He moved as quickly as he could, but when the device went off, the force of the explosion thrust him forward. Somehow, he didn't lose his grip on West, and the two slid forward.

*   *   *

As Sean and Rachel McEnany scrambled down the hallway, they stepped out to see Phil Lucena positioned behind the kitchen counter for cover and in a position to fire on the intruders. The couple joined him.

The three watched as a group of attackers stepped onto the deck. The leader moved to the locked doors.

Lucena asked, "How long will those doors and windows last?"

Sean had installed a kind of Plexiglass that was both bullet and explosive resistant – to a point, of course. He replied, "Looks like we're going to find out."

The six dark figures on the deck began firing with their submachine guns at the door and windows.

Sean, Rachel and Lucena each moved in small ways revealing their discomfort in waiting for the eventuality that the clear shielding to the room would give way.

And then the explosion from down the hallway seemed to rock the entire house.

Lucena's head shot around.

And even though the windows in the living room were starting to crack and buckle, Sean said, "Go."

Lucena nodded, and moved past Rachel and Sean.

The explosion had ripped apart walls, and part of the flooring.

As Lucena approached, two attackers had their backs to him. They were eyeing the impact of the explosion on West and Grant. The fifth man was just emerging from the stairs.

Moving ever closer, Lucena raised his gun, pulled the trigger, and the shot penetrated the neck of the fifth man.

At the sound of that shot, the two other members of the assault team started to turn. But they never got a good look at their opponent. Lucena was practically on top of them, as he moved without hesitation. He squeezed off two more headshots, and Lucena was past the two men before their bodies settled on the floor.

Grant struggled to push himself up. His mind was swimming. On his hands and knees, he tried to clear his head by working to focus on some of the debris underneath him.

Lucena glanced at Grant while sliding next to his fiancée who was face down. The back of her shirt was ripped, and there were cuts on the backs of her legs and torso.

Lucena pleaded, "Jess, are you alright?" He placed his hands gently on her shoulders.

West groaned, and tried to push herself over. Lucena helped.

She said, "What the hell? Are these shitheads dead?"

Before Lucena answered, the sound of shattering glass came from the front of the house, followed by much louder submachine gun fire.

Grant muttered, "Crap." He grabbed his Glock, forced himself to his feet, and said to Lucena, "You'll be the last defense, if needed." He took a deep breath and moved toward the gunfire. Grant knew that he was about to step into a situation whereby he, and probably Sean and Rachel, would be seriously outgunned.

As that calculus was running through his head, Grant looked down at one of the dead assailants, spotted a belt, and found a spark of hope in what was attached. He tossed aside his Glock.

In the living room-kitchen area, Sean and Rachel were left hoping that blind shots from behind the counter would hit someone.

She said, "This is ridiculous," and popped up firing. Rachel hit one target, and the man fell. But as she began to refocus on another target, two projectiles ripped along her upper right arm. She spun and dropped to the kitchen floor.

Sean jumped to her side, "Rachel?"

She rolled and looked up. "They're not deep. I'm okay."

Sean looked at his wife doubtfully, but then his eyes moved beyond his wife.

Two small round metal spheres flew out from the hallway.

Sean managed to lean forward, trying to cover as much of Rachel as he could.

The first two grenades thrown by Grant created dual explosions that not only ripped up a good chunk of the living room, but tore apart an attacker, and sent another flying backward.

The three other attackers were staggered.

Grant then stepped forward, and tossed two more grenades into the other half of the living room. That killed two more of the intruders, and sent the team leader, Jason Cox, into unconsciousness.

As Grant stood swaying, he looked down at Sean and Rachel. He saw the blood, and asked, "Shit. Are you alright?"

Rachel responded, "I really am." And with the help of Sean, she got to her feet and leaned on the counter. "You two need to make sure these guys are finished."

Sean looked warily at her, but with Grant, he proceeded to start surveying the damage to make sure no additional threats existed.

*   *   *

As Sean and Stephen were assessing matters in the former living room, West had gotten to her feet. Lucena was slowly guiding her in the direction of the kitchen.

A bedroom door opened, and Jennifer stepped out. She covered her mouth at the sights around her.

Lucena said, "Stephen is in the living room or kitchen."

Jennifer asked, "Are you two okay?"

Lucena nodded, and Jennifer turned to go find Stephen.

West whispered, "Or what's left of our living room and kitchen."

Lucena smiled weakly.

As they stepped carefully around debris and openings in the floor, Lucena spotted movement on the staircase to his left.

Before West could possibly know what was happening, Lucena shoved her forward. As she fell to the floor and skidded, one of the attackers plunged through the doorway with a knife in hand. He hit Lucena, and drove him into the wall.

Lucena stayed focused on the weapon, and managed to get one hand on the man's wrist and the other on the fingers that held the tactical knife.

The two tumbled to the floor, with the attacker landing on top of Lucena. The mercenary used his position and weight to push the knife down, and the blade began to penetrate Lucena's left cheek.

Despite the pain, Lucena tightened the grip on his opponent's fingers, and pulled his other hand away.

The blade moved another couple of centimeters into the cheek.

Lucena took his now free right hand, reached up and drove his thumb onto the attacker's left eye. He pushed the thumb further in, with his four other fingers wrapped around the side of the man's head, forming a brutal grip.

The pain and surprise led to the attacker releasing the knife.

Still gripping the attacker's eye socket, from which blood freely flowed, Lucena gained control of the knife with his left hand. He plunged the blade into the neck of his adversary, in the same place as the bullet earlier had struck the man.

After a brief scream and jerking motion, death came.

Lucena shoved the body off, and went to West. She already was crawling to him, and they fell into an embrace.

He whispered, "Thank God, you're alright."

She replied, "I was just thinking the same about you."

Chapter 13

The ten members of the assault team moved carefully – Uzis at the ready – toward the tipped-on-its-side SUV.

Inside the vehicle, Driessen was still strapped into his seat by the safety belt. He was looking down at Caldwell, who was stirring.

From the back seat, Chase Axelrod declared, "Shit."

Driessen asked, "Who's able to move?"

Semmler said, "Kent's on me. He's breathing but unconscious."

Axelrod replied, "And I'm on top of Kent and Brooke. Trying to reposition to reach the door."

Driessen said, "Move faster because I'm betting that whoever did this isn't done." He looked out the front window. "Shit. In fact, I can see at least one of these assholes moving toward us. And it looks like he's carrying a submachine gun." Driessen felt inside his jacket. "I can reach my Glock."

As the attackers cautiously moved toward the SUV, Due Tran was sprinting from the CDM building toward the wall running along the front of the property. In his hand was an Israeli IWI Negev NG7 machine gun, with the magazine belt. The new wall bordering the property had standing posts every 30 feet that an individual could climb up on to see over the wall and hedges – a precautionary option that the current situation showed to be a necessity.

Tran easily moved his slender frame up onto one of the small stands.

During practice firing sessions, the NG7 had become something of a favorite for Tran. He unleashed the rapid fire rounds on the five assailants with their backs to him, and each fell to the ground.

The other five – two in front of the SUV and three on the opposite side – turned their attention in Tran's direction.

The two men in front of the SUV didn't have much of a chance. They tried to raise their weapons, but were quickly mowed down.

However, the other three successfully dove behind the SUV for cover.

Tran stopped firing, and clearly was waiting for the attackers to emerge from cover.

But inside the SUV, Driessen had unbuckled, and moved himself right below the driver's side window. He hit a button and the window slid open. He started to undo his crouch, and then heard the three assailants, now below him, talking about how they would handle "the fucking guy with the machine gun."

With his Glock in hand, Driessen launched himself up and through the window. He slid along the door. Suddenly looking down on the final three assailants, he calmly deposited a shot into the tops of two men's heads, and when the third looked up, Driessen's shot entered the man's gaping mouth, and exited out the back of his skull.

After a few seconds of silence, Tran called out, "Are you guys okay?"

Driessen called back, "Good as can be expected. I think." He looked over his shoulder at Tran standing on the other side of the wall, and added, "Thanks, Tran."

Due Tran smiled, gave a thumbs-up, and replied, "My pleasure."

From inside the SUV, Caldwell called out, "Thanks to both of you. Now get us the hell out of here."

Chapter 14

At the end of the conflict at the house and hearing from Tran how things went down at the Sandcastle, Sean McEnany called a friend at the FBI, urging her to get their people to each location in order to take over from the local police.

After he hung up, the lone attacker who survived began to move and groan.

Sean stepped in close and let the man know that local law enforcement would not be involved. In his raspy voice, he presented Jason Cox with two options. "Don't cooperate, and you'll find yourself in an ungodly location likely for the rest of your days, as selected by friends in the CIA. Cooperate fully, and I can guarantee that the CIA can make you disappear to a far more comfortable place."

Nearly two hours later, Cox had more than cooperated. The man was in the know as the head of Victoria Wilsey's security teams, and due to the fact that the two slept together on a frequent basis.

McEnany then called Tank Hoard.

After hearing what McEnany had promised Cox, Hoard commented, "You're lucky that he gave us this much."

"Please, let's not play this game."

"You're right. We want her."

"Well, considering that the CIA has been pursuing a ghost for years, and it turns out the ghost is at least partially in the open and working with many of the people who want her apprehended or dead, I assume you would want her very badly."

"Yeah, I imagine there will be more than a few British politicians who will feel very uncomfortable when discovering the two lives of Victoria Wilsey." He paused and then said, "Listen, we need to act quickly. Can you and CDM do it?"

"Sure. When?"

"Now."

"That means our price is going to be higher than usual."

"Given the importance of this, I'm tempted to say 'Name your price.' But I'm not *that* stupid."

"You, in effect, just did say that."

Hoard noted, "By working with Charlie, I think you're developing a sense of humor, Sean."

McEnany didn't respond.

Hoard continued, "If you can get to L.A., I'll have a boat ready to get you to Santa Catalina Island."

"Text me the details about the boat."

After getting patched and sewn up by the FBI, Stephen, Jennifer, Rachel, Jessica and Phil had been gathered around Sean listening in on half of the conversation. After filling in the group on what they might have missed, McEnany said, "I can arrange for a helicopter and pilot to get us to L.A. It'll take a couple of hours."

Lucena, with his face sewed up and bandaged by an FBI medic, declared, "I'm going."

West, whose cuts up and down her back also had been treated, said, "Me, too." She looked at Phil, and before he could protest, she explained, "There's no way in hell that I'm not going with you on our wedding day. Somebody's got to keep you safe, so we can get to the church on time."

The next call by Sean was to the Sandcastle. When that call ended, Grant pulled Sean to the side. "I'm going and you're staying."

"You're out of your mind, *Pastor*."

"Tell me that you don't want to stay with Rachel."

Her gunshot wounds were not life threatening at this point, but they had run deeper than Rachel initially thought or had let on.

Grant continued, "I've got this. Coordinate with Due, and take care of your wife."

A half-hour later, Grant was climbing into a helicopter with Paige Caldwell, Charlie Driessen, Jessica West, Phil Lucena, and Chase Axelrod. Each had changed clothes – wearing casual clothes that would fit in on Santa Catalina Island – and carrying a backpack or shoulder case with assorted weapons.

Caldwell and Grant sat next to each other. She asked, "Jennifer okay with this?"

"She saw that Sean needed to be with Rachel. So, yeah, I think she was good with it – well, as far as things like this go given that she's married to a pastor."

"Yeah, I get it. You know, we were able to have a real heart-to-heart at the Pebble Beach spa. Just she and I. We got into a bunch of stuff."

"Excuse me? What happened at the spa?"

Caldwell looked at Grant, smiled, and said, "Oh, never mind. Nothing you'd find interesting."

Chapter 15

Sean McEnany's contact supplied the helicopter ride from Hollister Municipal Airport. Tank Hoard not only procured a boat to take them from the mainland to Santa Catalina Island, but the boat owner also had a convenient helipad.

The helicopter descended to a pad that rested on a hill above Santa Barbara, adjacent to a French-style mansion.

The aircraft set down and as the group exited, Grant watched a man emerge from the stone home. He was tall and thin, moved smoothly, and had a goatee and wavy brown hair with specks of gray. The man said, "Welcome. My name is Van Sharp, and I understand, from a mutual friend, that you need a lift to Santa Catalina Island."

As Sharp shook hands with each person, Paige Caldwell did introductions. She then said, "Thanks for your help, Mr. Sharp."

"Glad to do it, and please call me 'Van.'"

Grant looked closer at the man.

Sharp? Van Sharp? The movie director?

Sharp pointed in the direction of a white Cadillac Escalade.

As the SUV drove down the long driveway and through the opened gates, the helicopter took off, and headed north.

Fifteen minutes later, the CDM team, plus Grant, stepped onto a Kereon high-speed yacht. The two crewmembers had the 88-foot vessel ready to castoff.

While moving out of the harbor, Sharp proudly explained that the Kereon was of "Italian design and craftmanship," and its structure was "lightweight, and it's actually made of carbon and kevlar, and meant for speed." As the yacht approached open waters, he concluded, "I make this trip regularly, and we'll have you disembarking in less than a half-hour."

As the yacht accelerated smoothly on the calm waters and in the morning sunshine, Sharp's guests grabbed seats in various spots.

Caldwell, Grant and Sharp congregated in the main cabin.

Grant asked Sharp, "You're Van Sharp, the director, right?"

"I am."

"Oh, no," interjected Caldwell.

Sharp looked startled.

Caldwell said, "That wasn't directed at you, Van. Pastor Grant, here, *really* loves classic movies."

Grant added, "Guilty as charged, and your family" – he looked at Sharp – "is Hollywood royalty."

Sharp replied, "I'm not sure there's anything like Hollywood royalty, at least, not anymore, but thank you." He looked closer at Grant, adding, "But I'm wondering what I should respond to – the fact that you appreciate films or that you were just called 'Pastor Grant.' Let's take the second. What is a pastor doing with some former CIA types?"

"I'm former CIA, and now I'm a Lutheran pastor. Of course, my interest is piqued given that you're one of Hollywood's most successful directors, and yet, here we are on board your yacht at the behest of the CIA."

Sharp smiled wryly. "I don't think we have enough time to explore either of our stories, but I would like to do so one day."

"Same here," said Grant.

*   *   *

West and Axelrod were seated outside in the back of the yacht.

Axelrod – an African-American man who grew up in a tough Detroit neighborhood, was a college football star, mastered multiple languages, and came to CDM via Sean

McEnany – leaned back, and took in a deep breath of ocean air. He then asked, "You up for this?"

West answered, "Yes, but the body will be glad when it's over."

"Speaking of when this will be over" – he glanced at his watch – "are we going to make it to the church on time?"

She smiled, and said, "Depending on how things go, we have a chance. But either way, we've at least got most of the wedding party and the pastor with us."

Axelrod smiled. "Good point."

"And Phil and I don't leave for Hawaii until tomorrow."

"Another point in your favor."

West paused and then said, "Thanks again for being in the wedding party."

"You're two of my favorite people on the planet. It's great that you're getting married, and I can be part of it like this. Well, maybe not *exactly* like this."

*　　*　　*

Driessen and Lucena sat in the U-shaped sitting area toward the front of the Kereon.

"We've done this before – on the water and still tracking down the same person," declared Driessen.

"Weather's a hell of a lot better."

"True." Driessen said. He looked at the water and sky. "And this time, we know who we're going after."

A few moments of silence passed, and Lucena asked, "Does it bother you that Wilsey had Oakes murdered, and that she tried to have us and the people in our lives killed, but we're supposed to bring her in alive?"

Driessen stared at Lucena for a few seconds, and then responded, "I thought I was supposed to ask questions like that, or perhaps even your soon-to-be wife. But you?"

Lucena simply stared back.

Driessen added, "I understand why Tank wants her alive. But I won't be disappointed if Wilsey gives us no other option than to put a bullet between her eyes."

Chapter 16

As the yacht moved into the harbor, cruising by the Catalina Island Casino theater, Grant mentioned the wedding in passing.

Sharp said, "Wait a minute. Two of your people are supposed to be married this afternoon?"

"That's right – at a church in Santa Cruz. The question is time, including how quickly we can get back there."

Without hesitation, Sharp declared, "Take care of business, and I'll not only get your people back to my house, but I'll have *my* helicopter waiting."

Grant looked at Sharp, and said, "I think we just might take you up on that. Thanks very much."

Caldwell added her thanks, and within five minutes, the CDM group was off the yacht, and walking up the tight streets of the small, seaside town.

Each had a concealed Glock and tactical knife. West and Caldwell, however, also each had a long thin case over a shoulder with a Swiss SSG550 sniper rifle inside.

While they were in the air earlier, Sean McEnany had gathered and communicated the details of Wilsey's house and surrounding area. Being that Wilsey hadn't heard from Cox or anyone else from her assault teams, the CDM group had to assume that security would be beefed up, that is, if Wilsey hadn't already fled. That meant having options in trying to neutralize security in order to acquire their target. The parkland above and to the right of Wilsey's house provided two excellent options.

The group paused a couple of streets away from the Wilsey home. Caldwell went right, and West left. As those two moved to find the right positions, Grant, Axelrod,

Driessen and Lucena broke into pairs, and surveyed the streets approaching the home.

Word came via the small, two-way communication earpiece devices from Caldwell first, and then from West. Each was in position.

Driessen said, "Let's do this."

While the Wilsey home was large in terms of square footage, with three levels if one counted the expansive rooftop patio, it was much like the other homes in Avalon. That is, it basically sat right on the street, and had little spare grounds around the building itself.

Grant and Axelrod hid not far up the street on one side of the house, while Driessen and Lucena did the same on the other.

Caldwell was sprawled on the ground looking through the scope of her rifle. She reported, "I've got two guards, Wilsey, and perhaps her son, Adlai, on the roof. Wilsey and her son seem pretty relaxed at a table, and the guards are positioned to be able to look down on the street."

West, similarly spread out with a rifle and peering through the scope, said, "Confirmed. It also looks like the two guards are carrying machine guns."

Driessen commented, "Great." And then continued, "Okay, green light."

Caldwell's shot struck one of the guards, whose body fell over the short wall.

West had the other guard in her sights, and achieved the same result.

As Grant and Axelrod, and Driessen and Lucena approached the front of the home from each side, the guards' bodies struck the stone ground.

With his Glock 20 drawn, Grant stepped around one of the bodies.

Let's hope the other guards head up to the roof to protect their boss. Lord, be with me, with us.

There were four more guards inside the house, and they did in fact start moving to get to Wilsey on the roof.

Caldwell and West's following shots were precise, meant to try to pin Wilsey and her son in one position on the roof, rather than actually killing them.

At the sounds of gunfire at the front door's lock, and then Axelrod kicking the door in, two of the guards reversed course, heading down to stop the ground-based intruders.

*   *   *

The two guards who continued ascending reached the top of the circular stairs. One pulled the door open to the rooftop patio, but paused before going out. He watched where the gunfire was hitting.

Wilsey looked in his direction from underneath the table next to her son. She called out, "Well?"

The guard replied, "They don't want you killed. They're herding you, keeping you on the roof."

Wilsey looked back skeptically.

"Ma'am, please trust me."

She didn't move.

The guard told his partner to stay in position, and watch for anyone getting past the others in the house. He then took a deep breath, and launched himself into the open, moving haphazardly toward Wilsey.

The fire from Caldwell and West danced around him. But when he reached the table, and slid next to Wilsey and Adlai, the shots landed a bit farther away.

The guard pointed to where the shots were now hitting. "See what I mean?"

Wilsey nodded, and said, "Yes."

"Okay, let's go then."

Wilsey, her son and the guard formed up a tight, three person circle, and started to move together.

Watching through the scope, West declared, "Oh, fuck this." She steadied her weapon, held her breath, and then as she released the air in her lungs, pulled the trigger.

Part of the guard's skull exploded, with blood, bone and brain matter splattering on the faces of Victoria Wilsey and Adlai.

* * *

After busting in the front door, Axelrod and Grant proceeded with some caution. But Lucena and Driessen were moving more quickly, basically pushing past the others.

Alright. That's how we're playing this.

Grant's senses were further heightened. The open floorplan of the home gave the four an advantage. It turned out to be easy to spot the two guards as they began to descend the stairs. While one guard managed to get off a shot, the concentrated response from Lucena, Driessen, Axelrod and Grant gave them no chance.

Lucena now was in the lead, moving by the fallen guards, turning down the hallway leading to the circular staircase that went to the rooftop area. He leaned in, looked up and spotted the backside of the guard who was staring out the door.

Lucena aimed his weapon skyward, and called out, "Hey!"

The man turned, and looked down. It was the last thing he would see in life. Lucena's shot entered the man's head via his eyeball. The target tumbled forward, and awkwardly hit the turning staircase's railing and stairs, until he came to rest at Lucena's feet.

Lucena then led the other three up the circular stairs. He stopped and looked outside. A body was sprawled out on the floor between himself, and Wilsey and her son, who were back under the table.

Lucena said, "House is secure. Paige and Jess, hold your fire."

Hearing him through their earpieces, each replied, "Roger that." And they watched via their scopes.

Lucena and Driessen, with weapons trained, approached Wilsey and her son.

Grant and Axelrod scanned the rooftop just to verify that all was, in fact, secure.

Driessen ordered, "Show us your hands, and get the hell out from under that table."

Victoria and Adlai Wilsey followed his instructions.

While Lucena, Grant and Axelrod had their guns trained on the two, Driessen checked them for weapons. He then told them, "Sit down."

Grant noted that Wilsey's son clearly was nervous, perhaps even frightened. However, Victoria Wilsey seemed completely at ease. In fact, when sitting down, she rather casually crossed her legs.

Lucena stepped closer, with his gun now inches from Victoria Wilsey's face. "You murdered Jeff Oakes. You tried to murder my friends and my fiancée. Tell me why I shouldn't just pull the trigger."

Wilsey stared at Lucena dispassionately. She then shrugged, and said, "Do as you like. It matters not to me now. I have failed."

Adlai said, "Mother?"

She said with annoyance and dismissiveness, "Never mind, Adlai."

Adlai Wilsey's expression was immediately transformed.

At the same time, Grant had never seen such depth of anger on Phil Lucena's face.

No one moved on the rooftop.

Grant finally said, "Phil, please don't do this."

And then Jessica West spoke from a distance, still watching through her scope. "Stephen is right, Phil. Please, don't. She's not worth it, and I know you, you'll never forgive yourself."

Lucena relented. He lowered his weapon, and backed several steps away, while still looking at Wilsey.

Driessen then stepped forward, and placed the barrel of his gun on Wilsey's forehead.

"Charlie, what the hell?" Grant asked.

She still looks so indifferent.

"What is it, Grant? Why can't I just pull the trigger? Like this bitch, I have little to lose."

Now, Caldwell spoke from afar. "You know that's not true."

It was Grant's turn to add, "Listen to Paige. She's right."

Driessen didn't move, however.

Lucena stepped to Driessen's side, placed a hand on his shoulder, and said, "Hey, I need my best man. Today and beyond."

Driessen grunted and lowered his gun. He looked at Lucena and said, "Ah, now that's the Phil Lucena we all know."

Lucena smiled, and then looked at Wilsey. "Besides, maybe when the Agency is done with her, they'll want someone to dispose of her."

Driessen said, "Yeah? Sign me the fuck up."

Grant took Adlai Wilsey by the arm, and started directing him to the door leading off the rooftop. Axelrod did the same with Victoria Wilsey. But she stopped and looked at Lucena. "You're getting married to Miss West?"

He didn't answer.

"I know you are. That's why I chose this time to seek my revenge for you murdering my husband. I wanted to take it all away from you and then kill you."

"That wasn't murder. You and your husband? Arms dealers. Selling shit to the worst of the worst. He deserved what he got, and you deserve what you're about to get. Probably, you deserve worse."

Wilsey shrugged once more. "Here's my thought for your wedding: You should hope for a fraction of the complete love that Bertram and I had."

Lucena responded, "I pray that what Jessica and I have is nothing like whatever it is that you and your husband possessed. It's quite clear that you have no idea what love and marriage are about, but then again, what else would any of us expect from someone such as yourself? After all, you're an egomaniacal sociopath."

Adlai Wilsey, staring at his mother, spoke up. "He's right. And you're not as smart as you think you are. What happened to your fanatical talk about safeguards and not allowing anything to be traced back to you? These shits are here because you were fucking Cox, and told him too much."

Victoria Wilsey slapped her son's face with as much strength as she could muster. One of her nails drew blood. "You ingrate."

"And you are a stupid bitch in the end." He turned to Grant and said, "Get me the hell away from her."

Grant obliged, and Axelrod dragged Victoria away.

West said into her communication device, "Wow, that was interesting. And, babe, 'egomaniacal sociopath.' Nice."

That put a small smile on Lucena's face.

Caldwell cut in, "I just spoke to Tank. We need to ship Wilsey and her son back to the mainland, and he'll have some people ready to take them. Also, he contacted the FBI to take over the house scene."

Grant added, "Now, we're going to see if Van Sharp can get us to the church while there are still guests there. I'll contact Jennifer and have her keep Pastor Gibson updated. He can make an announcement. If that's alright with the happy couple?"

"Thank you, Stephen," responded Lucena with renewed politeness.

West added, "Yes, that would be ideal."

Chapter 17

As Van Sharp's helicopter descended toward the open grassy area next to Trinity Lutheran Church, the wedding guests were gathered just outside the church doors.

Looking out the window, West asked, "Phil, are those our wedding guests ... cheering and applauding?"

"Seems so." He squeezed her hand.

The welcome continued after the helicopter landed, and everyone disembarked.

Melissa Ambler was out front in greeting the couple. After exchanging hugs, Ambler said, "I'm so glad you're all okay. Listen, we have everything set for you two to get cleaned up and changed. Follow me."

Jennifer and Stephen hugged, and exchanged a quick kiss.

Jennifer said, "Thank God, you're alright. Everyone else?"

"All good."

She smiled, and said, "I brought your liturgical duds to change into for the wedding. Everyone's been great waiting. Pastor Gibson was masterful."

Twenty minutes later, as Jessica was being walked down the aisle, Grant wasn't just amazed that he was able to pull himself together – *That's mostly Jen* – and how cleaned up Paige, Chase, and Charlie were, but he was downright astonished by Phil and Jessica. No one looked exactly as planned. For example, Jessica's long blond hair fell over her shoulders and down her back, rather than being set up and curled as originally intended. And she had bandages and bruises on her back and legs.

Phil actually had a slight shadow on his face, not being able to shave, given the lack of time and with his sewed up and bandaged cheek. But the two radiated joy, without a trace of being hindered by the day's events.

A bit later, Grant looked down from the pulpit at the couple and smiled. He then gazed out at those in the pews, and began:

> Grace and peace to you from our Lord and Savior Jesus Christ. Amen. Get ready. I'm tossing out my prepared homily for today. Don't worry, Jessica and Phil, it'll make sense. I hope.
>
> If you wonder what love and marriage are supposed to be about, I'm going to relay two very different views that I recently observed. One view holds that marriage is just about a man and a woman, and nothing else matters. Whatever makes the couple happy is more than okay; in fact, it's essential. The marriage is exclusively about the couple, and all else is gauged or measured as to how it affects that marriage. This is a perversity, often with grim consequences. Unfortunately, though, I'm not sure how out of the ordinary it is.
>
> The second view recognizes that at the center of a marriage, of course, is a man, a woman and their love. But it also understands that a marriage touches others in many ways, and that marriage requires sacrifice for each other and for others.
>
> In Ephesians 5, St. Paul takes a lot of flak in the modern world for using the word "submit." As I said during Jessica and Phil's premarital class, ultimately, we should let Scripture, rather than the current culture, define the term. And in fact, we each submit to other Christians for the sake of Christ, and the Church submits to Christ. Christ and his relationship to the Church is about sacrificial love. In our lives, that most

commonly points us to forgiveness and even unconditional love. But sometimes, it points us to be willing to make the ultimate sacrifice for others.

So, marriage isn't just about one man and one woman. It often has far-reaching implications. Keep in mind that the most important moment in human history was when Christ laid down his life for us, for His Church, taking on our sins, and offering love, forgiveness, redemption and salvation. St. Paul actually invites the married couple to be an image, if you will, that points us toward the relationship between Christ and His Church.

Grant looked directly at Jessica and Phil, and said, "I saw that perspective on marriage recently as well."

He then continued with the sermon and the service.

After the ceremony, pictures were taken on the stone and grass area outside the church. In the background, the sunset created an inspiring mix of yellow, orange and blue on the Pacific Ocean and in the sky.

Stephen and Jennifer stood holding hands, taking in the entire moment. He asked, "So, you and Paige had massages together at the Pebble Beach spa?"

Jennifer replied, "Oh, did she mention that?"

"She did. What did you two talk about?"

Jennifer said, "Nothing you'd find interesting."

"That's exactly what Paige said."

Jennifer laughed, and said, "Did she, really?"

Stephen smiled and shook his head.

A few seconds later, Pastor Gibson walked up next to them, and said, "Nice homily."

"Thanks," replied Stephen. "Nice sunset."

"Told you."

For Your Further Interest...

• If you want to know what happened at the University of Notre Dame, read *Under the Golden Dome*.

• If you're curious about what happened on the mission to Jordan that Jessica West references, read *Persecution*.

• If you want to know more about the challenges faced by Jessica West, Melissa Ambler and Brooke Semmler on the beach volleyball sands, please check out *Shifting Sands*.

• Find out how Due Tran reappeared in the lives of Stephen Grant and Paige Caldwell in *What's Lost?*

• If you're wondering how matters played out for Mike Vanacore, Melissa Ambler and Stephen Grant, please check out *Murderer's Row*.

• The story of Zhu Gao can be found in *Deep Rough*.

Acknowledgments

Thank you to the members of the Pastor Stephen Grant Fellowship for their support:

Silver Readers

Gregory Brown	Sue Lutz
Chris Comerford	Daniel Provost
Mark Friis-Hansen	Steven Muther
Robert Rosenberg	Sue Kreft
Gary Wright	

Bronze Readers

Michelle Behl	Tony Hunt
John Manweiler	Peter Meier
Beth Nagy	Terry Merrill
Audrey Williams	

Supportive Readers

Fredericka Richter DeBerry	James Fryckman
Linda Gerke	

I love and appreciate my family. As always, I'm grateful for Beth's support and editing prowess. I admire my two sons, David and Jonathan, including for their wisdom and senses of humor. And my daughter-in-law, Mikayla, and my granddaughter, Phoebe, are simply awesome.

Any and all shortcomings in my books are all about me, and no one else. Thanks for the encouragement. And as long as someone keeps reading, I'll keep writing. God bless.

Ray Keating
July 2023

About the Author

Ray Keating is a novelist, an economist, a nonfiction author, a podcaster, a columnist, and an entrepreneur.

At this point, Keating has penned 18 Pastor Stephen Grant thrillers and mysteries (with more on the way) – *Warrior Monk*, followed by *Root of All Evil?*, *An Advent for Religious Liberty*, *The River*, *Murderer's Row*, *Wine Into Water*, *Lionhearts*, *Reagan Country*, *Heroes and Villains*, *Shifting Sands*, *Deep Rough*, *The Traitor*, *Vatican Shadows*, *Past Lives*, *What's Lost?*, *Persecution*, *Under the Golden Dome*, and now *For Better, For Worse*. He also has begun the Alliance of Saint Michael series, with *Cathedral*.

Among recent nonfiction books are *The Lutheran Planner: The TO DO List Solution*, *The Weekly Economist II: 52 More Quick Reads to Help You Think Like an Economist*, *The Weekly Economist: 52 Quick Reads to Help You Think Like an Economist*, *Behind Enemy Lines: Conservative Communiques from Left-Wing New York* and *Free Trade Rocks! 10 Points on International Trade Everyone Should Know*.

In addition, Keating is the editor/publisher/columnist for DisneyBizJournal.com, and hosts three podcasts. He was a columnist with RealClearMarkets.com, and a former weekly newspaper columnist for *Newsday*, *Long Island Business News*, and the *New York City Tribune*. His work has appeared in many periodicals, including *The New York Times*, *The Wall Street Journal*, *The Washington Post*, *New York Post*, *Los Angeles Daily News*, *The Boston Globe*,

National Review, The Washington Times, Investor's Business Daily, New York *Daily News, Detroit Free Press, Chicago Tribune, TheHill.com, Touchstone* magazine, *Townhall.com,* and *Cincinnati Enquirer.*

Never Miss a Book by Ray Keating – Join the Pastor Stephen Grant Fellowship!

Never miss a book by Ray Keating by joining the Pastor Stephen Grant Fellowship. Become part of a community of fellow readers, and open additional communications with Ray. By joining the Pastor Stephen Grant Fellowship, you also help make sure that more books are coming!

Check it all out at
www.patreon.com/pastorstephengrantfellowship.

There are a variety of levels to join, including...

Bronze Reader

You receive all new novels and short stories FREE and earlier than the rest of the world. In addition, your name is included in a special "Thank You" section in forthcoming novels, and you have access to the private Pastor Stephen Grant Fellowship Facebook page, which includes journal entries from Pastor Stephen Grant, insights from other characters, regular recipes from Grillin' with the Monks and other characters, periodic videos and Q&A's and thoughts from Ray Keating, and more!

Silver Reader

All of the benefits from the Bronze level, plus you receive two special gift boxes throughout the year with fun and exclusive Pastor Stephen Grant merchandise.

Live Club

All the benefits from the Silver level, plus you'll be on a monthly live ZOOM call with Ray Keating, author of the Pastor Stephen Grant thrillers and mysteries. Ray will talk a bit about the books – including what's coming – and/or writing in general, but the key is that you can get involved with the conversation with Ray and other readers. Ask questions, offer suggestions, and so on. It's fun and informative.

Book of the Month Club

1) Receive a FREE book EVERY MONTH written and signed by Ray Keating. Included are Pastor Stephen Grant thrillers and mysteries (new books in the month of release), other fiction books, and Ray's nonfiction books. If you request, Ray will personalize his signing to a person of your choosing.

2) Take part in the monthly live ZOOM call with Ray Keating, author of the Pastor Stephen Grant thrillers and mysteries

3) Two special gift boxes throughout the year with fun and exclusive Pastor Stephen Grant merchandise.

4) Your name included in a special "Thank You" section in forthcoming novels.

5) Access to the private Pastor Stephen Grant Fellowship Facebook page, which includes journal entries from Pastor Stephen Grant, insights from other characters, regular recipes from Grillin' with the Monks and other characters, periodic videos, various thoughts from Ray Keating, and more!

Gold Reader

All the benefits of the Book of the Month Club level, plus your name or the name of someone you choose to be used for a character in **one** upcoming novel.

Ultimate Reader

All the benefits from the Book of the Month and above Gold Reader level, plus your name or the name of someone you choose (in addition to the one named under the Gold level!) to be used for a **major recurring character** in upcoming novels.

Enjoy All of the Pastor Stephen Grant Adventures by Ray Keating!

Paperbacks and Kindle versions at Amazon.com

Signed books at raykeatingonline.com

• *Under the Golden Dome: A Pastor Stephen Grant Novel*

Pastor Stephen Grant and his wife, economist Jennifer Grant, are invited to a conference at the University of Notre Dame. While they look forward to speaking at the same gathering, unexpected dangers materialize, fueled by distorted, political impulses among some in the Church. Defending religious freedom isn't limited to a conflict of ideas, as the struggle turns deadly.

• *Persecution: A Pastor Stephen Grant Novel*

While the charge of "persecution" gets tossed about rather casually, Pastor Stephen Grant and some of his closest friends and associates get a close-up, bloody view of what it truly means to be a modern-day martyr. From the White House to the Vatican, and from Russia to the Middle East, the action is unrelenting and the suspense is palpable. Can Grant and his former CIA colleagues act in time to save innocent lives?

• *What's Lost? A Pastor Stephen Grant Short Story*

From the pages of his own journal, Pastor Stephen Grant tells a riveting mystery involving deception, betrayal, sacrifice and friendship, along with plenty of action and questions about what we truly can know about others. Grant takes us on a personal journey across decades and around the world, from Long Island to Vietnam. This is the second Pastor Stephen Grant story told from Grant's own viewpoint, unfolding each day in the pages of his journal.

• *Past Lives: A Pastor Stephen Grant Short Story*

Torn from pages of his own journal, Pastor Stephen Grant tells about threats, murder and puzzling people from his past. It's a compelling mystery involving action, unexpected turns, lost innocence, sought-after perspective, and twisted revenge. This is the first Pastor Stephen Grant story told from Grant's own viewpoint, unfolding each day in the pages of his journal.

• *Vatican Shadows: A Pastor Stephen Grant Novel*

More than 500 years ago, two men – Jan Hus and Martin Luther – tried to bring about change in the Catholic Church. They suffered, with one burned at the stake. Could a modern-day pope transform these reformers from heretics to heroes in the eyes of the Catholic Church? Shadowy figures inside and outside the Vatican oppose Pope Paul VII's efforts, and stand willing to do anything to stop him. For help, the pope turns to Stephen Grant, a Lutheran pastor, former Navy SEAL and onetime CIA operative.

For Better, For Worse 85

- **The Traitor: A Pastor Stephen Grant Novel**

Stephen Grant – former Navy SEAL, onetime CIA operative and current pastor – looks forward to a time of prayer and reflection during a retreat at a monastery in Europe. But when he stumbles upon an infamous CIA traitor in a small village, Grant's plans change dramatically. While a debate rages over government secrets and the intelligence community, a deadly race for survival is underway. From a pro-democracy demonstration in Hong Kong to the CIA's headquarters in Langley to a monastery in France, the action and intrigue never let up.

- **Deep Rough: A Pastor Stephen Grant Novel**

One man faces challenges as a pastor in China. His son has become a breakout phenom in the world of professional golf. The Chinese government is displeased with both, and their lives are in danger. Stephen Grant – a onetime Navy SEAL, former CIA operative and current pastor – has a history with the communist Chinese, while also claiming a pretty solid golf game. His unique experience and skills unexpectedly put him alongside old friends; at some of golf's biggest tournaments as a caddy and bodyguard; and in the middle of an international struggle over Christian persecution, a mission of revenge, and a battle between good and evil.

- **Shifting Sands: A Pastor Stephen Grant Short Story**

Beach volleyball is about fun, sun and sand. But when a big-time tournament arrives on a pier in New York City, danger and international intrigue are added to the mix. Stephen Grant, a former Navy SEAL, onetime CIA operative, and current pastor, is on the scene with his wife, friends and former CIA colleagues. While battles on the volleyball court play out, deadly struggles between good and evil are engaged on and off the sand.

• *Heroes and Villains: A Pastor Stephen Grant Short Story*

As a onetime Navy SEAL, a former CIA operative and a pastor, many people call Stephen Grant a hero. At various times defending the Christian Church and the United States over the years, he has journeyed across the nation and around the world. But now Grant finds himself in an entirely unfamiliar setting – a comic book, science fiction and fantasy convention. But he still joins forces with a unique set of heroes in an attempt to foil a villainous plot against one of the all-time great comic book writers and artists.

• *Reagan Country: A Pastor Stephen Grant Novel*

Could President Ronald Reagan's influence reach into the former "evil empire"? The media refers to a businessman on the rise as "Russia's Reagan." Unfortunately, others seek a return to the old ways, longing for Russia's former "greatness." The dispute becomes deadly. Conflict stretches from the Reagan Presidential Library in California to the White House to a Russian Orthodox monastery to the Kremlin. Stephen Grant, pastor at St. Mary's Lutheran Church on Long Island, a former Navy SEAL and onetime CIA operative, stands at the center of the tumult.

• *Lionhearts: A Pastor Stephen Grant Novel*

War has arrived on American soil, with Islamic terrorists using new tactics. Few are safe, including Christians, politicians, and the media. Pastor Stephen Grant taps into his past with the Navy SEALS and the CIA to help wage a war of flesh and blood, ideas, history, and beliefs. This is about defending both the U.S. and Christianity.

• Wine Into Water: A Pastor Stephen Grant Novel

Blood, wine, sin, justice and forgiveness... Who knew the wine business could be so sordid and violent? That's what happens when it's infiltrated by counterfeiters. A pastor, once a Navy SEAL and CIA operative, is pulled into action to help unravel a mystery involving fake wine, murder and revenge. Stephen Grant is called to take on evil, while staying rooted in his life as a pastor.

• Murderer's Row: A Pastor Stephen Grant Novel

How do rescuing a Christian family from the clutches of Islamic terrorists, minor league baseball in New York, a string of grisly murders, sordid politics, and a pastor, who once was a Navy SEAL and CIA operative, tie together? *Murderer's Row* is the fifth Pastor Stephen Grant novel, and Keating serves up fascinating characters, gripping adventure, and a tangled murder mystery, along with faith, politics, humor, and, yes, baseball.

• The River: A Pastor Stephen Grant Novel

Some refer to Las Vegas as Sin City. But the sins being committed in *The River* are not what one might typically expect. Rather, it's about murder. Stephen Grant once used lethal skills for the Navy SEALs and the CIA. Now, years later, he's a pastor. How does this man of action and faith react when his wife is kidnapped, a deep mystery must be untangled, and both allies and suspects from his CIA days arrive on the scene? How far can Grant go – or will he go – to save the woman he loves? Will he seek justice or revenge, and can he tell the difference any longer?

• *An Advent for Religious Liberty: A Pastor Stephen Grant Novel*

Advent and Christmas approach. It's supposed to be a special season for Christians. But it's different this time in New York City. Religious liberty is under assault. The Catholic Church has been called a "hate group." And it's the newly elected mayor of New York City who has set off this religious and political firestorm. Some people react with prayer – others with violence and murder. Stephen Grant, former CIA operative turned pastor, faces deadly challenges during what becomes known as "An Advent for Religious Liberty." Grant works with the cardinal who leads the Archdiocese of New York, the FBI, current friends, and former CIA colleagues to fight for religious liberty, and against dangers both spiritual and physical.

• *Root of All Evil? A Pastor Stephen Grant Novel*

Do God, politics and money mix? In *Root of All Evil?*, the combination can turn out quite deadly. Keating introduced readers to Stephen Grant, a former CIA operative and current parish pastor, in the fun and highly praised *Warrior Monk*. Now, Grant is back in *Root of All Evil?* It's a breathtaking thriller involving drug traffickers, politicians, the CIA and FBI, a shadowy foreign regime, the Church, and money. Charity, envy and greed are on display. Throughout, action runs high.

• *Warrior Monk: A Pastor Stephen Grant Novel*

Warrior Monk revolves around a former CIA assassin, Stephen Grant, who has lived a far different, relatively quiet life as a parish pastor in recent years. However, a shooting at his church, a historic papal proposal, and threats to the pope's life mean that Grant's former and current lives collide. Grant must tap the varied skills learned as a government agent, a theologian and a pastor not only to protect the pope, but also to feel his way through a minefield of personal challenges. The second edition of *Warrior Monk* includes a new Introduction by Ray Keating, as well as a new Epilogue that points to a later Pastor Stephen Grant novel.

Cathedral: An Alliance of Saint Michael Novel

The Start of a New Series from Ray Keating

Paperbacks and Kindle versions at Amazon.com

Signed books at raykeatingonline.com

Cathedral: An Alliance of Saint Michael Novel is Ray Keating's first installment in the Alliance of Saint Michael series.

The Alliance of Saint Michael brings together men and women with varied backgrounds and talents to work covertly against the two most significant threats to Christianity and civilization at the dawn of the 1930s - communism and fascism.

In Moscow, the Cathedral of Christ the Saviour is going to be obliterated to make way for the Palace of the Soviets. The Alliance of St. Michael readies itself for its first mission – find and salvage a rare item of great significance from the cathedral before the building is lost.

The Weekly Economist: 52 Quick Reads to Help You Think Like an Economist

The Weekly Economist II: 52 More Quick Reads to Help You Think Like an Economist

Both Books by Ray Keating

Paperbacks and for the Kindle at Amazon.com and Signed books at raykeatingonline.com

If you don't have a degree in economics, how do you figure out what actually makes economic sense and what doesn't? Ray Keating, a leading economist on small business and entrepreneurship, offers help with *The Weekly Economist: 52 Quick Reads to Help You Think Like an Economist* and *The Weekly Economist II: 52 More Quick Reads to Help You Think Like an Economist*.

Whether via CNBC, CNN, FOX, websites, or other outlets, many assertions regarding the economy and economic policy are presented that leave people wondering what's accurate and what's not. That's especially the case when declarations by one talking head are conflicted by the next one. *The Weekly Economist* series offers quick reads on topics essential to thinking clearly on economics, or apply sound economic principles to hot topics.

Free Trade Rocks! *10 Points on International Trade Everyone Should Know*

by Ray Keating

Paperback and for the Kindle at Amazon.com

Signed books at raykeatingonline.com

While free trade has come under attack, Ray Keating lays out in clear, simple fashion the benefits of free trade and the ills of protectionism in *Free Trade Rocks! 10 Points on International Trade Everyone Should Know.*

Tapping into his experiences as an economist, policy analyst, newspaper and online columnist, entrepreneur, and college professor, who taught MBA courses on international business and entrepreneurship, Keating explores and explains in straightforward fashion 10 key points or areas that everyone - from entrepreneurs and executives to students and employees to politicians and taxpayers - needs to understand about how trade works and how free trade generates benefits for people throughout the nation, around the world, and across income levels.

Behind Enemy Lines: Conservative Communiques from Left-Wing New York

by Ray Keating

Paperback and for the Kindle at Amazon.com

Signed books at raykeatingonline.com

Enjoy this wide-ranging collection of columns and essays from Ray Keating covering faith, economics, politics, history, trade, New York, foreign affairs, immigration, pop culture, business, sports, books, and more. Keating is a longtime newspaper and online columnist, economist, policy analyst, and novelist. In these often confusing and contradictory times, Keating describes his brand of conservatism as traditional, American and Reagan-esque, firmly rooted in Judeo-Christian values, Western Civilization, the Declaration of Independence, the U.S. Constitution, and essential ideas and institutions such as the Christian Church, the intrinsic value of each individual, the role of the family, freedom and individual responsibility, limited government, and free enterprise and free markets. There's a great deal to enjoy, learn from, agree with, get annoyed by, appreciate, reflect on, roll your eyes over, and argue with in this book that offers perspectives on where we are today, where we've been, and where we might be headed.

Visit DisneyBizJournal.com

News, Analysis and Reviews of the
Disney Entertainment Business!

DisneyBizJournal.com is a media site providing news, information and analysis for anyone who has an interest in the Walt Disney Company, and its assorted ventures, operations, and history. Fans (Disney, Pixar, Marvel, Star Wars, Indiana Jones, and more), investors, entrepreneurs, executives, teachers, professors and students will find valuable information, analysis, and commentary in its pages.

DisneyBizJournal.com is run by Ray Keating, who has experience as a newspaper and online columnist, economist, business teacher and speaker, novelist, movie and book reviewer, podcaster, and more.

Free Enterprise in Three Minutes Podcast with Ray Keating

This podcast provides three-minute (give or take a few seconds) answers to important questions about free enterprise, the economy, business and related issues. Ray Keating cuts through the economic mumbo-jumbo, tosses aside the economic mistakes often made in the media and in political circles, and quickly gets at economic reality. Who says free enterprise and economics have to be mind-numbing? That's not the case with *Free Enterprise in Three Minutes with Ray Keating.*

Listen in and subscribe at Apple Podcasts, on Buzzsprout, at Amazon.com, or wherever you listen to your podcasts.

"Chuck" vs. the Business World: Business Tips on TV

by Ray Keating

Paperbacks and for the Kindle at Amazon.com

Signed books at raykeatingonline.com

Among Ray Keating's nonfiction books is *"Chuck" vs. the Business World: Business Tips on TV*. In this book, Keating finds career advice, and lessons on managing or owning a business in a fun, fascinating and unexpected place, that is, in the television show *Chuck*.

Keating shows that TV spies and nerds can provide insights and guidelines on managing workers, customer relations, leadership, technology, hiring and firing people, and balancing work and personal life. Larry Kudlow of CNBC says, "Ray Keating has taken the very funny television series *Chuck*, and derived some valuable lessons and insights for your career and business."

If you love *Chuck*, you'll love this book. And even if you never watched *Chuck*, the book lays out clear examples and quick lessons from which you can reap rewards.